ENTERTAINING THE EARL

Vows in Vauxhall Gardens, Book 2

Daphne Quinn

ARE YOU SIGNED UP FOR DRAGONBLADE'S BLOG?

You'll get the latest news and information on exclusive giveaways, exclusive excerpts, coming releases, sales, free books, cover reveals and more.

Check out our complete list of authors, too!

No spam, no junk. That's a promise!

Sign Up Here

www.dragonbladepublishing.com

Dearest Reader;

Thank you for your support of a small press. At Dragonblade Publishing, we strive to bring you the highest quality Historical Romance from some of the best authors in the business. Without your support, there is no 'us', so we sincerely hope you adore these stories and find some new favorite authors along the way.

Happy Reading!

CEO, Dragonblade Publishing

Additional Dragonblade books by Author Daphne Quinn

Vows in Vauxhall Gardens
The Lady of the Lamps (Book 1)
Entertaining the Earl (Book 2)

CHAPTER ONE

M ISS SUSANNAH LYTTLETON was never happier than when she had a book in her hands and some peace and quiet to enjoy it.

She devoured every novel she could get her hands on, regularly begging her father for new additions to the Lyttleton library. It was not as if Papa did not have the funds, after all. But he did think there were better things for his daughter to be doing than reading whenever she could.

It was on such a day, when the air was turning cooler and autumn was upon them, that Susannah found herself curled up on a chair before the fire, enjoying Miss Austen's latest tome. The author's name had only become common knowledge after her death, and this second posthumous novel had only just been published. Susannah had been eagerly awaiting it, desperate to get her hands on a copy.

She didn't notice her father entering the parlor until he was before her, sighing and commenting, "Reading again, Susannah?"

She tried to ignore the censure in his voice. "It's awfully good, Papa," she said, although she knew he had no interest in reading. She was not sure where her love of books had come from, considering neither of her parents ever spent any time reading. Well, not exactly. She supposed her mother perused the gossip columns—if one could really call that *reading*.

"Well, I have some news for you," he said, strolling over to the port decanter on the table and pouring himself a healthy glass.

Susannah sat upright, not wanting to be criticized for her deportment, and waited for whatever news her father had to share. She doubted it would be something she was particularly interested in, for her parents' news tended to be about social events: who had wed, who was caught in scandal, and who was having a child. All topics that did not interest Susannah.

"We're to host a guest for the Season."

"Why?" was Susannah's first question. She did not enjoy the social Season, which was due to start shortly and was the reason they were in London. She played her part, attending dances and musicales and smiling when her mother told her to. But she knew she was plain-looking, and her interest in books was not something that endeared her to the men in society. It was no surprise to her—and probably to her parents, either—that she had not received an offer of marriage in the three seasons she had been out in society. She knew it was probably to her disadvantage that their family's status had only been elevated enough for her to first attend the London Season at the grand old age of twenty-two.

"Because we have been asked to," her father said, his tone a little short. "And it is a great honor."

"Who is she?" Susannah asked, assuming that her mother had been asked to sponsor some young lady's debut, now that they were mixing with the upper echelons of society. With her father having made his fortune, rather than having inherited it, it had taken the ton a while to accept the Lyttletons—but it seemed now that they were a firm fixture of the London Season. So it was no huge surprise that some lesser-known family, perhaps without a matriarch, wished for Mama to present their daughter.

"Not she," her father said, looking pleased with himself. "He. The Earl of Bourne, to be precise."

"Why would an earl wish to stay with us?" Susannah asked, her bluntness as usual seeming to offend Papa. But it was surely a fair question; why should someone with such a title want to stay with Mr. and Mrs. Lyttleton, no matter their wealth or status in society?

"Because," her father said through gritted teeth, "he wishes to become reacquainted with London society, and we are well-placed to help him."

"Are we?" Susannah asked, before quickly correcting herself. "Of course, we are."

In that, Susannah thought her father might have a point. Having aspired to the ton for so long, her parents had both studied their behaviors extensively and raised Susannah to have every skill of a refined young lady. "Why is he so…unacquainted with London society?"

Papa took the seat opposite her and lit a cigar. "He has been on an extended tour around Europe. He inherited while he was away, I believe—and now that it's time for him to return, he and his aunt—whom your mother and I are acquainted with—feel he needs a little guidance before being thrust into the Season."

"And so he is to stay with us," Susannah surmised.

"And so he is to stay with us," Papa said, his voice full of glee. "He can attend functions with us, and if he is unsure about anything, we will be there to support him. It is a great honor, Susannah."

"Yes, indeed," Susannah said, feeling her agreement was what was desired at that moment.

"You will need to entertain him," Papa said, blowing out a ring of smoke. "You must not hide away in your books, Susannah. This is an opportunity for the whole family. We will show him the Season at its very best—and that includes time at home with the family."

Susannah inwardly groaned. She could picture him now—some elderly duke with a receding hairline and no wit or humor. And it wasn't just that she had to smile and be polite at a ball or a dinner—here, in the safety of her own home, she would have to entertain him, to put down her beloved books and pretend to be something she was not.

For the whole Season.

It was a very displeasing thought, but she tried not to let that show on her face, for her father was clearly excited by the prospect.

"You cannot hide away in books forever, Susannah. It is time you took your place in the real world—and think seriously about marriage and your future."

Her parents were rather obsessed with her future. She knew she ought to be preoccupied with the notion of whom she would marry, too—but she struggled to muster up much enthusiasm for the idea.

She was happy enough here, in their London townhouse, and even more so at their country home, where she could hide away more easily with her books. There were fewer social expectations in the country, and far more space, making it harder for her parents to stumble upon her reading and make their disapproval known.

Susannah was very happy to *read* about love and marriage, but in the real world, she rather thought matrimony would interfere with the time she enjoyed by herself.

And anyways, it was beside the point; nobody had ever asked her. And she doubted they ever would—so what was the use in obsessing over it?

CHAPTER TWO

THE SEA WAS not particularly rough, yet still Colin's stomach churned. The passage back to Britain was long and arduous, and if he had forgotten why he had not made the return journey in many years, this voyage was a stark reminder.

As much as he loved to travel, his body was not built for sea voyaging. He certainly would never have made it in the Navy, for even short journeys made him cast up the contents of his stomach.

But there was never going to be any need for him to join the Navy. He had always been wealthy and titled, and now that he was the Earl of Bourne, his position in society was set.

He just had to come back and take it.

"Do you need anything, my lord?" asked one of the lads who was always running around the ship fetching and carrying.

Colin shook his head.

"No, thank you," he managed to say, just before turning back to the sea and gripping tightly to the edge of the boat.

If he was to be sick, he would rather nobody saw him.

It had been seven years since he had last returned to Britain's shores and two years since he had gained the title of 'earl'. His father had already been long dead by the time Colin heard the news all the way in the Americas, and there had seemed no reason for him to hurry back. The estate was in good hands, with the staff his father had employed keeping things running smoothly.

Then came a letter from his aunt, informing him that the very capable man of business who had run his father's affairs had died, and she was concerned for the future of the Bourne estates. That letter had made him rethink.

He couldn't stay abroad forever. He was an Englishman—he needed to step up to the responsibility. As much as he wished he could stay away.

And so, there he was, hating every moment aboard this ship, sailing back to London for that quaint tradition of society's Season. His aunt was, it seemed, concerned that his reputation had been damaged by being away for so very long, and so she insisted that being seen in London, before returning to deal with the estates, was the right thing to do.

The boat lurched, and Colin's grip grew tighter, his knuckles going white. There was no sight of land yet. He had lost track of how many days they had been at sea and could only hope that there were not too many more to go. And then, he vowed, he would never set foot on a boat again. He would accept that he would only ever see the shores of England, for traveling this way was truly intolerable.

Whether he would remember that vow once his feet were safely on dry land was an entirely different matter.

He had left London at the tender age of eighteen, intent on seeing the world—and that he had certainly done. From the mountains of Europe to the Great Lakes of North America to the caves of the Mediterranean. He had seen and wondered at so much of the world—and yet what he was returning to was a complete unknown.

The London Season. At eighteen, it had not been something he was interested in. He had gone out and drunk and gambled with his friends, but he had avoided balls and other society functions where he would be expected to pay court to some debutante.

But if he was going to take his place in society, the Season was where he needed to be. He supposed he would need a wife, too—for the earldom required an heir. But there was no rush. He was only five-and-twenty. This year, he simply wished to reacquaint himself with London and how things were done. He did not wish to make a fool of himself, upon his return to society. After all, the expectations of an earl were rather different in England than they were on the Continent or even farther afield.

"Dinner is served, my lord," another lad said, but even the thought of food made Colin nauseous.

"I do not think—" he began, but then the rocking motion of the boat became too much for him to handle, and he cast up what little he'd eaten for lunch over the side of the boat.

The lad tutted sympathetically and then went about his business, leaving the sorrowful earl alone.

Things would be better on dry land. His aunt had arranged for him to stay with a family she knew, so that he would not enter the Season completely unprepared. He wasn't sure how much he wanted company every single day, but he knew his aunt meant well. And besides, it would be rather less daunting to return to a ballroom in the company of people who regularly attended such places, rather than to walk in as a titled, tanned stranger and face the inevitable whispers and gossip alone.

When he had left England's shores, he had been the son of an earl with an unpalatable reputation. He was returning as the new earl, and with little known about him, he was sure the gossips would be focusing on his father's disreputable behavior.

There had been no love lost between Colin and his father. The two had barely known each other. But nonetheless, Colin was the Earl of Bourne now—and he wanted to do it right.

It was hard to imagine what England could have to offer him, however, after everything he had seen and done during his travels.

CHAPTER THREE

SUSANNAH SAT IN the window seat, alternating between reading a few more pages of her beloved book and watching London society as it passed by her window.

She had no desire to be out there, but she did sometimes enjoy watching as the ton paraded down Mayfair, conversing and laughing, trying to attract attention, or flirting and giggling with some new beau. Often, a young couple would be accompanied by one of their mothers, or maids trailing behind to chaperone. Susannah liked to make up stories in her head about them—where they were going, who they were, what they wanted in life.

One day, although she had never admitted it aloud, she wanted to write her own novel—just like Miss Austen.

But she knew without asking that her father would never approve. He did not like anyone knowing or reminding him that he had earned his fortune. He had not dirtied his hands, of course—but he had overseen large shipments of goods which had given him the riches he so desired, if not the title.

He expected more from his daughter—wanted more for her. And so he certainly would never accept her earning money through something so common as writing.

Susannah sighed and turned back to her book. She didn't care about the money, in truth—other than that it might be a sign that people valued her work. The Lyttletons had more money than Susannah would ever know what to do with. Her dowry was larger than that of the daughters of viscounts and earls. She just wanted to write, and for people to read what she had written.

Just as she was getting engrossed in the story in the pages before her, the parlor door opened—and she looked up to see her father standing there, looking exceptionally pleased with himself.

"Susannah, I would like to present to you our very special guest, the Earl of Bourne."

As her father stepped to one side to allow the gentleman behind him into the room, Susannah stood, put down her book, and smoothed out her skirts. It was important to her father that she made a good impression on this earl, that she showed their family in the very best light, and so she meant to make an effort.

But when the Earl of Bourne stepped into the room, all words left her head. She was usually quiet, preferring to think and read rather than socialize, but she had never been accused of being empty-headed. In that moment, however, her mind felt entirely blank.

She had been expecting an elderly gentleman, with a receding hairline, or a powdered wig, perhaps carrying a cane. But the Earl of Bourne was nothing like she had imagined. He was tall, far taller than her father, with a head full of blond curls and the most dazzling blue eyes she had ever seen. His skin was more tanned than was fashionable in London society, but it only made him more handsome.

He was, without a doubt, the most attractive gentleman Susannah had ever met—and for some reason, his presence made her blush and forget how to speak.

"Lord Bourne," her father said, looking rather puzzled at his daughter's silence. "Please allow me to present my daughter, Miss Susannah Lyttleton."

The earl bowed his head, and, after a glare from her father, Susannah remembered the need to curtsy.

"A pleasure to meet you, Lord Bourne," she managed to squeak out.

"The pleasure is mine, Miss Lyttleton," he said, and his voice sent a ripple through Susannah, one she did not quite understand.

"As I told you, Lord Bourne will be here for the entirety of the Season. I'm sure you will make him feel welcome."

"Yes, Papa," she said, finding it easier to avoid the earl's eyes and simply address her father. At least that way, she could get some words out.

"And please, Lord Bourne, make yourself entirely at home. Anything you need, just ask."

"You are most kind," the earl said. "I am very grateful for your hospitality. I must admit, returning to London after so many years away is rather daunting. I am grateful for your guidance."

Looking overjoyed that the earl was so appreciative, Mr. Lyttleton showed him from the room, leaving Susannah mercifully alone.

For a moment, she stood absolutely still as her heart began to return to its normal rhythm. Once her limbs had unfrozen, she took a seat in an armchair and took a deep breath.

What on earth had that been about? Never in her life had the appearance of a gentleman caused her to react so. And had she not been in the presence of handsome gentlemen before? None came to mind. Of all the gentlemen she had danced with in her three Seasons on the marriage mart, not a single one had made her feel so giddy. And not a single one could compare in looks to the Earl of Bourne.

She reached for her book, but she could not focus on the words written on the page.

She was rather disturbed by the way she had reacted. This was surely not how a logical, sensible woman responded. And the man would think she was a simpleton. He was to stay in their house for the Season, and she could not possibly allow herself to become so empty-headed every time she was in his presence. It simply would not do.

Susannah drummed her fingers on the book and told herself that it was simply a reaction of surprise, because she had expected an old man. Yes, that was it. Her body had just reacted due to the unexpectedness of Lord Bourne. Next time, she would be prepared and wouldn't respond in such a foolish way.

CHAPTER FOUR

MR. LYTTLETON WAS a pleasant enough gentleman, with a very fine home in the heart of Mayfair and a real eagerness to please. His wife was polite but fairly quiet, and his daughter barely seemed to say a word.

Colin thought that she was probably afraid of him, although he was not rude enough to ask. She was clearly unwed, or she wouldn't still live with her parents, and he wondered whether it was crippling shyness that stopped her from being successful in finding a husband. She had looked like a frightened little mouse when he had come into the parlor, and had barely been able to look him in the eye.

He very much hoped that Mr. and Mrs. Lyttleton were not planning to encourage a match between them. He was sure she was a pleasant enough woman, but he really was not looking for a wife yet. And surely, when he did, she would need to be someone who was comfortable in society, considering his rank. He was not experienced in socializing among the ton himself; he needed a wife who was more capable.

After the tour of the house, he retired to his bedchamber for some peace and quiet and watched the busy London streets from his window. He owned his own townhouse in the city—although he still thought of it as his father's—but it had been closed up for many years. Even before the old earl had died, he had not been well enough to visit London, and so the staff had been let go, and the place had fallen into disrepair. It was something he would rectify once the Season was over and he had reintegrated himself into society. But for now, it was far easier to stay with the Lyttletons, attended to by their excellent staff, while he reacquainted himself with London society.

⫸⫷

"I HAVE MADE no secret of the size of your dowry this year," Papa said, upon finding Susannah holed up in the library reading, hours before the first ball of the Season. "So I expect you will have far more suitors this year."

"Thank you, Papa," she said, because she knew it was the expected answer. But in truth, the thought of someone asking for her hand because he would become rich by doing so turned her stomach. She didn't particularly want to get married. She was already five-and-twenty, but her father had only been considered rich and important enough to mingle with the upper echelons of society for the last three years, and so she had not been paraded around endless Seasons before then.

Nevertheless, there had been no proposals of marriage—and she hadn't particularly been surprised. She knew she was plain, with her mousy brown hair and brown eyes, and that her interest in fictional worlds was rather dull to most people.

Then there was the fact that she had no title, nor a great family name to ease her way in society. The ton had long memories, and, if she ever did have children, she imagined it would be several generations before her father's lack of pedigree was forgotten.

But now it seemed her father was making it clear that she came with a large fortune—and undoubtedly, that might be enough to make men in need of money overlook her background and her plain features.

It was not how she wanted to be married, but she was not

sure what choice she had. She was quite happy to remain at home for the rest of her days, reading and living with her parents. But she doubted they would consider that an acceptable option.

"Ah, there you are, Susannah," her mother said, seeming to float into the room. The daughter of the younger son of a viscount, her mother had probably expected to marry someone titled, but when her own father had gambled away his fortune, a rich suitor had been more important. Susannah had heard gossip about this over the years, but never heard any specifics from her parents. And perhaps they were a good example of how marrying for money could work out; even if it hadn't been a love match, they always seemed fairly happy together. Susannah had never heard them arguing, and her mother always made sure that the Lyttletons were well represented in society.

"Reading again, are you?" she said with a sigh, and Susannah closed her book and laid it in her lap, feeling frustrated that her peace had been disturbed, and trying not to make it apparent on her face. "You must begin getting ready for the ball."

"But we have hours still," Susannah argued. She had been hoping for more time with her book before she was forced into society.

"This is the first ball of the Season, Susannah," her mother said disapprovingly. "It is vital you make a good impression, if we are to find your match this year. Now, I have selected your gown, and Louise will be along shortly to pin your hair. Everything must be perfect tonight, do you understand?"

"Yes, Mama," Susannah answered, putting down her book sadly and following her mother from the room.

COLIN HADN'T EXACTLY been a social recluse during his travels, but things were different on foreign shores. From what he remembered of English society, people were quick to judge and rarely forgave or forgot errors.

When he had last attended a function on these shores, he had been a lad of eighteen—and not an earl. Things were certainly different now, and he couldn't help but worry he wouldn't live up to the title.

The Lyttleton valet had offered to help Colin dress for the ball, as he had not yet engaged in one of his own. He was grateful, for the man clearly knew exactly what was expected and it seemed possible he was one of the finest valets in the ton.

The man looking back at him in the mirror looked very different from the one he was used to seeing. His blond curls were tamed into submission, and his cravat was tied so perfectly around his neck that he could hardly believe it hadn't been done with magic.

"Do you require anything else, my lord?" the valet asked after brushing over his coat sleeves with a clothes brush.

"No, thank you," Colin said, resisting the urge to loosen the cravat. He felt as though he couldn't quite catch his breath—but that was surely just nerves. He would feel better once he had a drink in his hand.

During his travels, things had always been less formal. He hadn't even always told the people he spent time with that he was now an earl. It was rather nice, socializing without people worrying about addressing him correctly, and without him having to worry about living up to the title.

"Very good, my lord. I believe the carriage will be here shortly."

Colin waited in the foyer with Mr. Lyttleton for the two Lyttleton women to descend the stairs. He was truly grateful that he did not have to enter the ballroom alone, even if his companions were people he had only met the day before. He had been gone so long that he had no friends left in London. No one he could call on to make him feel a little less out of place.

Which was, he assumed, why his aunt had set up this situation. He would visit her after the ball and discuss her concerns about the estate, and his reputation, having been away for so long. She would undoubtedly have heard whatever gossip arose from tonight's ball—although she very rarely attended such events herself—and she would surely have an opinion on how he had performed.

He only hoped he wouldn't let her down.

At the sound of footsteps on the stairs, Colin looked up and was rather surprised to see how different Miss Susannah Lyttleton looked. When they had been introduced earlier, she had worn a plain, practical day dress, and her mousy brown hair had been pulled back in a style that made her look much older. But now, in a green dress far more suited for dancing, with a neckline that was almost daring, and her hair pinned neatly in a crown atop her head, she looked… well, she looked almost pretty. He felt rather uncharitable for thinking otherwise earlier.

He smiled at both Lyttleton women and bowed.

"Good evening, ladies. And may I say how beautiful you both look."

Mrs. Lyttleton wore a gown of lavender that flattered her, and she seemed quite confident in it. She smiled and thanked him for his compliment, taking her husband's arm.

Miss Susannah Lyttleton, however, didn't seem to know where to look. Her cheeks flushed bright red, and she tripped on the last step, nearly falling flat on her face. Colin jumped forward, catching her arm just in time and helping her right herself.

Her parents turned to see what the commotion was, and her mother sighed. "I swear, Susannah. Your head is in those books even when there are none to be seen. Please pay attention to what you're doing."

Susannah looked mortified and snatched her arm back before following her parents out to the carriage.

Colin was left with the distinct feeling that he had done something to offend her, even though he had no idea what it could be. Surely he shouldn't have let her fall on her face? And it wasn't as though she knew he thought she looked unexpectedly pretty. He wasn't foolish enough to say something like that out loud—so she couldn't possibly be offended by it.

It was a shame though, he mused, as they stepped into the carriage for the short journey to the ball, that her parents were so quick to judge her. He wondered if, without worrying about their remarks, she might have been a little more confident.

CHAPTER FIVE

SUSANNAH WAS SILENT during the journey to the Denman home, where the first ball of the Season was being held.

She didn't feel comfortable in the modern dress her mother had chosen for her, its neckline more daring than anything she had ever worn before. She had already been dreading the thought of men pursuing her solely for her dowry, and that was without the embarrassment of tripping down the stairs in front of Lord Bourne—and the mortifying situation of him having to catch her.

She was never so clumsy. When she was reading while doing other tasks, she might get distracted—but she was perfectly capable of walking downstairs without making a fool of herself.

It was his fault, she decided as the carriage rattled across the cobblestones. She had steeled herself to expect his presence, and she thought she had been doing well, not allowing her mind to turn to jelly—and then he had complimented her.

And she knew he was only being polite. Of course, she had heard him offer the same compliment to her mother. But still, his words took hold, and she had lost all sense yet again.

She could not allow this to keep happening every single day. Surely, at some point, she would grow immune to whatever power he held over her?

HE MUST HAVE danced with every young lady present, Susannah thought, for it was hours before he left the dance floor—not even stopping for refreshment. He was in great demand, and Susannah thought that was understandable. Most of the gentlemen of the ton were familiar faces, either not looking for a wife or already married.

The Earl of Bourne was new and exciting, and, of course, devastatingly handsome.

She tried not to watch him all night, for she knew no good could come of it, but there was little else for her to do. She was rarely asked to dance these days unless someone felt sorry for her, and so she stood with all the other spinsters and wallflowers, watching everyone else live their lives, fall in love, and waiting for the evening to be over.

There was a break in the music, and she lost sight of him for a moment. It seemed that her father's bragging about her dowry and her mother's insistence on a lower neckline had not vastly changed things for Susannah. Oh, there had been a gentleman or two who had looked her way, but she had only danced twice all evening, and no one had shown any serious interest. Perhaps her new packaging had intrigued some, but once they realized she was still Susannah Lyttleton underneath it all—rather plain, rather boring, with more common roots than they would have liked—that interest fell away.

Her mother stood beside her, wittering on about some lady's fan and how ostentatious it was, but Susannah wasn't really paying attention. Instead, she was wondering if she could sneak away and continue the novel she had stashed in her reticule.

Mama would be furious, of course—but Susannah thought it might be worth it to escape the boredom she currently felt. When, she wondered as the musicians picked up their instruments again after a brief refreshment break, would her mother stop insisting she attend such functions? Surely there was a point at which it became obvious that all of this was futile. Then, perhaps, she could be left alone with her books and spinsterhood.

But alas, it did not seem as though this Season would be the one. Her parents still held out hope—and while that was the case, she was sure she would be trussed up and paraded about at every event, whether or not there was any likelihood of success.

"May I have this dance, Miss Lyttleton?"

She had been so lost in her thoughts that she hadn't even noticed the Earl of Bourne approaching her until he was standing right before her, asking the surprising question.

Once again, Susannah's mind went entirely blank. There was not a word she could think to utter until her mother jumped in and replied, "Of course you can. How delightful."

Susannah did not know if he was asking from pity or obligation, and she tried not to care. She had been watching him dance with other young ladies all night, and she had to admit she'd rather wanted to dance with him too.

He took her hand and led her to the dance floor, and Susannah felt as though her whole body was on fire. Heat radiated from the point of contact, even though he wasn't even touching her bare skin but merely the satin of her glove.

She was sure everyone was staring at them—more likely, staring at him and probably wondering what on earth he was doing dancing with Miss Susannah Lyttleton.

"Do you not like to dance?" the earl asked, and it took a great deal of effort for Susannah to think of a sensible answer and force her lips to open in reply.

"I do enjoy it, Lord Bourne," she said, wondering why he thought such a thing. Perhaps it was because she had barely danced all night...but that was not exactly her choice.

"You don't look very happy to be on the dance floor," he said, and she met his sparkling blue eyes and couldn't help but smile back at him.

"I admit, it makes me nervous to have so many eyes upon me. I am not used to such...attention."

The earl laughed. "Nor am I."

She couldn't help but giggle. "Surely that cannot be true.

You're an earl, and you look like... Well, like you do..." She trailed off, heat rushing to her cheeks at what she had nearly said—at what she had implied. Of course, she presumed he was well aware of how good-looking he was, but she certainly hadn't intended to say it out loud.

If he noticed, he didn't comment, but simply shook his head. "You forget, Miss Lyttleton, that I have been used to a very different sort of life. Many of the people I've spent time with over the last decade haven't even known I'm an earl, or was in line to be one, let alone been impressed by such a thing. I'm certainly unaccustomed to having the interest of so many young ladies…and their mothers."

He raised his eyebrows, and Susannah had to smother another giggle. He was funny—funny and good-looking, and seemingly kind too, for he had asked her to dance. It seemed rather unfair for one man to have all three desirable traits, but he did.

No wonder all of society was fawning over him.

"You are a young earl, and unwed, you cannot be wholly surprised by their attentions," she said, pleased that she was managing to speak coherently before him.

"No, I suppose not," he said with a sigh. "I just did not expect it to be so…intense."

She nodded, as though she understood what he was saying, but she had never known the intense gaze of society. Even in her first Season out, no one had paid much attention to her, and even now with her well-publicized dowry and lower neckline, she still did not attract the attention of the men of the *ton*. So she could not understand what it was like to have people flocking around, even though she tried to empathize.

COLIN FELT DRAINED by the evening. Every time he had finished dancing, another group of young ladies had seemed to appear, and he did not want to appear rude by not asking any of them to dance. But if this was how the rest of the Season was to be, he didn't know how he was going to manage. He had expected some interest in his return, but not to have young ladies and their mamas pushing marriage options towards him at every turn.

Although he had been dancing for most of the night, it had not escaped his notice that the daughter of his hosts had barely danced at all. She was clearly very shy, and he wondered if it was that she didn't want to dance, or was simply not asked.

But as they danced, she spoke a little, and he found she had more to say than he had expected when faced with the silent young woman he had met in the library at the Lyttletons' London home. And he found himself wondering why she was not asked to dance more, and why she was not wed. She was not a great beauty, it was true, but she was not unappealing…and when she smiled, it lit up her face and transformed it.

And the topic which seemed to engage her the most was books.

"Are you reading anything interesting at the moment?" he asked her, having seen her reading both when he had arrived and again that morning.

"All books are interesting," she said, a smile playing on her lips. "But I am currently reading *Persuasion*, by Miss Austen."

"And are you enjoying it?" he asked.

"Immensely. Have you read any of Miss Austen's work?"

"Alas, I am afraid I tend only to read historical tomes, or accounts of travels…not fiction."

She tutted. "Gentlemen think that reading novels is not a worthwhile pursuit, something beneath them, but I am sure if you gave novels a try, you would find yourself pleasantly diverted. And perhaps you might learn a thing or two about yourself, and society."

She'd put more words in that single statement than all the rest she'd uttered since he'd arrived, and that made him stop to consider. Whatever his view on novels, they certainly mattered to her. Colin did not think he viewed reading novels as beneath him…it was just not something he had been particularly inclined to do. He frowned. "Well, whilst I am staying with you, you will have to recommend some of your favorites, and I shall see if I am enlightened by reading them."

"Oh," she said, her eyes widening a little. Had she expected him to be rude about the novels she loved so much? Or to refuse to listen to her recommendations? "Yes. I will."

The music came to an end, and Colin escorted her back to her parents, where a crowd of ladies had formed, all waving their fans and smiling in his direction.

He smiled back, but his heart wasn't in it. It was flattering, of course, to be at the center of such ardent attentions, but he rather longed to be somewhere else; somewhere on the continent, perhaps, where those around him either didn't know or didn't care that he was the Earl of Bourne, and where he didn't have to worry so much about living up to people's expectations.

SHE WATCHED HIM for the rest of the evening. He smiled at every lady, danced with as many as he could, and his companions always left him with a sparkle in their eye.

What must it be like, she mused, to be able to charm people like that? To have them hanging from your every word?

And yet she couldn't blame the young women who were fluttering their eye lashes at him and smiling behind their fans. He was charm personified; he even seemed interested in the books she was reading, and wanted recommendations. No man had ever asked her that before. She felt, for that brief period on the dance floor, as though she was finally being seen—and that was a heady feeling indeed.

CHAPTER SIX

VISITING VAUXHALL PLEASURE Gardens was one of Susannah's more preferred activities during the Season. Although there was still the expectation to dance and socialize with other young people, here were also entertainments she found far more enjoyable than the tittle-tattle: the fireworks, the cascade, the glass lanterns… All of it had an air of magic and set her imagination racing. When they had been before—though they did not go regularly, for while the gardens were popular, there was still a slight hint of scandal surrounding them—Susannah had always returned home full of ideas, ideas she desperately scribbled down.

Perhaps one day those ideas would become a novel—if she was brave enough. She doubted she would ever let anyone see her writing, and she wasn't sure if she had the confidence to write more than a scene here and there. For what if she found she was no good at it? She had loved books and reading for as long as she could remember, and it would break her heart to discover she did not have the skill with words that those she admired so greatly possessed.

"I think you will enjoy the Pleasure Gardens," her father said as their carriage made slow progress toward the dock where they would take a boat to the gardens. "Many improvements have been made since you last visited. They are quite spectacular."

"I have heard tales of the entertainments on offer," the earl said. "I look forward to seeing them. I must admit, my memory of the place is very sparse. I think I only visited once, many years ago. Do you like the gardens, Miss Lyttleton?"

Susannah had noticed that he often tried to draw her into conversation when she was sitting silently. She did not know if this stemmed from genuine interest in her opinions or perhaps some desire to prove that he could make her talk. Perhaps he was just one of those people who did not like silence.

"Susannah has only been twice," her mother said, jumping in before Susannah could answer. "While they are wonderful, that is rather enough excitement for a young girl, I feel."

Susannah stopped herself just in time from rolling her eyes. She had actually been on four separate occasions, although perhaps her mother wasn't aware of that, since two of those visits had been while she was out of town. She wasn't such a young lady anymore—she doubted very much that she would be corrupted by the excitement of an evening at Vauxhall.

But it would not do to disagree with her mother publicly, and so she simply said, "Yes. When I have visited, I have been quite intrigued by what they offer. And I rather wish to know how they can make the cascade look like water when it is made of metal. Quite ingenious."

Her mother sighed, as though young women should not be thinking about the mechanics behind an artistic display, but Susannah caught sight of the earl smiling and couldn't resist smiling back.

It almost felt criminal how much he put one at ease. Surely it would mean scores of girls with no hope of attracting him would fall in love with him this Season. And that hardly seemed fair. Yet he did not appear to be purposefully charming everyone; it was just his natural way.

She was sure that evening he would be as inundated with female attention as he had been at the Denman Ball earlier in the week. He was the shiny new penny—and how shiny he was.

Whereas she would stand on the fringes of society and watch as matches were made and people fell in love. She would watch him dance with all the women who were far more suitable than she. Because, whether or not he smiled and showed an interest, he was never going to look at her. Not seriously. She would never expect such a thing. But she would not become one of the many who fell for him and then mourned their loss at the end of the Season when he would surely announce a betrothal to a pretty young lady with a title and perfect breeding.

THERE WAS A hum of excitement in the air as they disembarked from the little boats that had brought them to the gardens.

Colin was keen to see them, though not so keen to submit himself to the same attentions he had endured at the Denman Ball. Yet hiding away from society was not an option. After all, the reason he had returned was to take his place, to ensure his estates were run properly, and to avoid any distasteful gossip about him or his title.

Hopefully, once it was clear he had no plans to take a wife in the near future, some of the attention would fade. When he was ready to find a wife, perhaps having all these options before him would be helpful—although, even then, he rather thought he would still feel overwhelmed by the attention.

But he had no need or wish to find a wife at present, and the sooner these women realized it, the better for everyone.

"They'll be lighting the lamps soon," Mr. Lyttleton said, hurrying them along. "It really is a sight to behold, especially when you haven't been in the city for so long."

Colin had seen some of the greatest sights in the world and felt privileged to have done so. But still, he appreciated this little corner of England and the spectacle prepared for the lords and ladies who attended.

A BELL TOLLED, and Colin turned to Miss Lyttleton. "Would you accompany me to the Cascade, Miss Lyttleton?" Colin asked, needing a break from the marriageable young ladies in the garden. The Cascade's nightly display had come at the perfect time.

Whilst they would certainly still hover, they were not generally rude enough to approach him if he was already speaking with another young lady.

In fact, that was what had given him the idea for the plan he was about to propose. He did not wish to be rude to anyone, he just wanted to be left alone—and he rather thought Miss Lyttleton felt the same.

"Of course, my lord," she said, with a glance to her parents to make sure that it was acceptable. Unsurprisingly, they looked thrilled by the prospect, and so they walked together towards the Cascade, where a crowd was already forming.

The spectacle was indeed impressive, and for a few moments they watched as the mechanical waterfall moved, accompanied by a surprisingly loud sound made to mimic running water.

"It's like magic, isn't it?" Miss Lyttleton said, raising her voice to be heard over the din.

"Yes," Colin agreed, finding himself mesmerized. He had seen many wonders on his travels, but this was certainly worth visiting.

"My parents don't understand my fascination with it," Miss Lyttleton said with a sigh. "But every time I have visited, I have to see it. I begged Papa once to stay later than he intended, because they hadn't yet unveiled it that evening."

Colin found himself feeling rather sorry for Miss Lyttleton. She seemed to be overlooked by everyone, her parents included. They did not seem to appreciate her interests at all. He would have assumed that it was far more interesting to converse with a daughter about novels and the workings of the Cascade, than it would have been to have a daughter who was only interested in fashion and gossip...but clearly they saw it as problematic.

"It is an experience indeed," he agreed. Beside him, a group of giggling young ladies seemed to be edging closer, and so he took Miss Lyttleton's arm and maneuvered them both a little further away.

She gasped as he touched her elbow, and he realized he should have said something before doing so, but he really just wanted to get away from the women waiting for him to ask them to dance.

"I have a favor to ask you," he said, quietly enough that those around should not be able to hear him, but he hoped loudly enough that she could.

She looked up at him, her brown eyes catching the light of the lamps and looking more the color of honey. They were wide, and for a moment he found himself staring into them, forgetting what it was he meant to say.

CHAPTER SEVEN

"LORD BOURNE?" SHE said in a breathless whisper, and he blinked and forced himself to focus on what he had wanted to ask her.

He cleared his throat. "I wonder…if we might act as though we have formed an attachment."

Her mouth formed an "o", but she did not say a word.

"I do not wish to marry this Season, but that does not seem to be filtering through to the ladies of the *ton*."

"So you wish to…pretend?"

"If we let people believe we have an…understanding, then I believe I will be left alone. When the time comes to dissolve it, you can of course break things off with me, and there will be nothing to tarnish your reputation."

They both watched the Cascade for several moments, until Colin realized he was still holding onto her arm and abruptly let go. *That* would certainly get people talking. Although, he supposed, if they were to pretend to be planning to wed, that was what they wanted.

"And what would I get from this arrangement?" she suddenly asked.

Colin paused. He had only really thought of it as being to his benefit, which was unfair of him—but he was sure she would find it useful, too.

"It will keep your parents from pushing you to attend functions and dance with every man there."

⟫⟫⟫⟪⟪⟪

SHE HAD NOT realized that he had noticed how little interest she had in the events her parents wanted her to attend—but clearly he was more observant than she had given him credit for.

"And then you could read to your heart's content."

Very observant indeed.

"My parents wish for me to marry. If I am seen with you...then my prospects, as meager as they are, will surely diminish further."

Colin shook his head. "No, I do not believe that is true. Men are always, for better or worse, more interested when someone appears out of reach—so you may find that you have more suitors, not fewer." He paused for a moment, and then added, "And I shall furnish your library with any book you wish for."

Susannah could not help but be intrigued by the proposition. She had never had an understanding with any young man, but she had seen enough of society to believe she could pretend well enough.

And while she had no great desire to marry, it was her parents' greatest wish—and so, if pretending to have an attachment to the handsome Lord Bourne would help with that...she supposed it would do no harm. If it meant she could be left alone to read, well, that would certainly make the Season more enjoyable. She could afford to purchase any book she wished, but the earl's offer was a thoughtful one. She thought he very well might be able to procure books she could not otherwise find.

"It would only be for the Season," Lord Bourne insisted when she still did not answer. "For once it is over, I plan to return to my estate in Kent and focus on ensuring everything is in order for quite some time."

Would she be able to convincingly pretend that a man like Lord Bourne could possibly be interested in her? Would society believe it? And could she manage to speak sensibly with him when, for some reason, one look from him seemed to make her heart race and her thoughts turn to mush?

"I'm not sure how believable it would be," she eventually managed to say.

Lord Bourne frowned. "You think I cannot act sufficiently to persuade the *ton*?"

Susannah laughed, because it was a ridiculous notion that it would be because of him that people did not believe the lie.

"It is not that, my lord. They will look at you, and they will look at me, and they will think something does not add up. They will not believe a man…like you…would show an interest in a plain girl like me."

She spoke the words calmly and factually, for they were something she had long since accepted. But it still hurt—just a little—to be forced to admit it, especially to such a handsome and kind man.

His eyes softened, and she looked away, feeling as though she might get lost in their blue depths. Just a look from him gave her that tugging sensation in the pit of her stomach that she did not understand but which she was sure could only lead to trouble.

"I am simply realistic," she murmured, although she did not know whether he heard her or if her words were lost to the sound of the Cascade in its final moments of the evening.

"Well, I disagree, but I will not argue with you. If that is your only argument against it, I think we should proceed."

No other argument came to mind, and so she found herself saying, as the Cascade finished for another evening, "Very well. We can try…"

The earl beamed. "Excellent. Then please allow me to escort you to the dance floor."

She felt like all eyes were on her as he led her onto the dance floor, but once the music began, she focused on him alone. The way he moved, the way he smiled, the way a blond curl sometimes fell in front of his face, causing him to run a hand through his hair to push it back.

She didn't need to pretend to be attracted to him, that was for certain. She just hoped people could believe that he was attracted to her…

CHAPTER EIGHT

"LORD BOURNE SEEMED to be paying you a lot of attention last night," Mama said as they sat in the parlor sewing before luncheon. She had a self-satisfied smile on her face, and Susannah avoided her eye, sure that her mother would be able to tell she was lying if she looked directly at her.

"Yes, he was," she agreed. No lie there at least—although she wasn't exactly being honest by withholding the reason why.

"He is a very handsome young man," Mama added, and Susannah managed to stab herself with her needle, and shoved her finger in her mouth before the blood dripped on the handkerchief she was embroidering.

"Do be careful, Susannah."

She was used to her mother's admonishments; sewing was not her forte. But perhaps, once her mother believed she had caught the attention of the earl, she would be allowed a little more freedom to sit and read...

"He has asked me to promenade with him, after lunch," she said, and was rewarded by a beam from her mother. "Once he has returned from seeing his aunt."

"What a turn of events," her mother said as she completed a perfect row of stitches. "Your father knew having the earl to stay would improve our social standing, but he never imagined... Make sure you are wearing one of your new day dresses, Susannah, and have Louise do something more flattering with your hair. He is the bachelor of the Season—you must make sure you keep his attention."

⟫⟫⟫⟭⟬⟬⟬

"AND HOW ARE things going, with the Lyttletons?" Aunt Elizabeth asked, as her butler poured the tea.

"They are very accommodating. How is it that you know them?" Colin asked.

"Mr. Lyttleton managed some very profitable investments for your late uncle, and Mrs. Lyttleton calls on me from time to time. I'm glad you are finding staying with them useful."

Colin reached for his teacup and took a sip, although the liquid was still far too hot. "I must admit, I had forgotten what London society was like. The intense interest in me...it is certainly helpful to attend functions with a family, rather than alone."

"As I thought. You are a very attractive possibility for the ladies looking for a husband. You cannot be surprised by their attentions."

He shook his head. "Not surprised, so much as a little overwhelmed. I am used to being Colin, not the Earl of Bourne."

Aunt Elizabeth tutted. "You have been the Earl of Bourne for many years, and simply shirking your responsibilities by pretending to be anything else."

"You know Father and I—"

"You had your disagreements, yes. I am not blaming you for the estrangement, but I am disappointed it has taken you so long to return, now that he is gone and you are the earl. You have responsibilities, Colin, you must not forget that."

"I am here. You told me the estate needed me, and I have returned."

His aunt crossed her arms and huffed. "I should not have needed to tell you to return."

Colin closed his eyes for a moment and took a deep breath, suppressing a sigh of frustration. He had never asked to be the earl, and he had returned as soon as she had bid him too.

The estate had managed for all these years; he wasn't so sure his presence was as essential as Aunt Elizabeth seemed to think.

"Your father certainly had his faults," Aunt Elizabeth conceded, "but he was always invested in the earldom, in the future of the title, in the productivity of the land."

Colin could not help but snort in disgust at this evaluation. "Oh yes, he was very attentive to the earldom. But what about Mama? Did he ever think of her?"

"Colin, there is no use raking up the past. I simply want you to step up to the duty that you were born to inherit."

"And I shall. But I have no wish to be like my father. The man had mistresses in every corner of London and probably a whole host of illegitimate children. You know my mother died of a broken heart—and for that, I can never forgive him, no matter how good he was at being the earl."

His aunt looked away, clearly not wishing to engage with the distasteful topic, and Colin sipped his tea to have something to do.

"I do not wish to argue with you, Colin. I am pleased that you have returned, and I think you will make a good earl once you have settled into the role."

"Thank you, Aunt," Colin said, forcing his voice to be polite. He supposed she couldn't help but have some loyalty toward her deceased older brother…but Colin did not feel that way.

The man might well have been a good earl, but Colin knew now that he had not been a good father, and he had not been a good husband. And he wanted to be better than him—in all areas of his life.

"I heard that you danced with Miss Lyttleton more than once at Vauxhall Gardens," Aunt Elizabeth said, changing the subject.

"You're very well-informed," Colin said, reaching for a biscuit on the plate before him.

Aunt Elizabeth shrugged. "I may not attend many functions now, but that does not mean I do not hear about them. You are aware, I am sure, what people will say if you are too attentive to her."

"I understand the implications, yes."

His aunt frowned, clearly surprised by his nonchalant attitude toward what she was suggesting. "She is a sweet girl, but rather plain, no? I would not imagine that she would catch your eye above all the other shining jewels the Season has to offer."

Irritation filled Colin's veins. The attachment they were portraying to the world might have been fake, but he did not like how overlooked Miss Lyttleton was. It seemed as though everyone wrote her off as dull and plain without giving her a second glance. And yet, when one conversed with her, she was rather intelligent. She had a quick wit, too, although it was often hidden by her shyness. And her eyes...her eyes seemed to have hidden depths that he had only discovered when he had held her gaze for a few moments too long.

"I am not planning to hurry down the aisle tomorrow, Aunt. You needn't worry yourself. But Miss Lyttleton is pleasant company. I plan to promenade with her this afternoon, once I have taken my leave of you."

⇥⟩⟩⟩⟨⟨⟨⇤

"How was your morning?" Lord Bourne asked as they strolled through St James's Park, Susannah's maid following behind.

"It was..." Susannah began. She had been going to say pleasant, for that was surely the expected response—but this relationship between them wasn't real, and so she thought she could be honest. It was easier to talk with him when they were walking, rather than seated opposite each other, because she couldn't focus on how he had dimples when he smiled, or how his eyes sparkled when she asked him about his travels. "It was rather dull, I'm afraid."

Lord Bourne chuckled. "I'm sorry to hear that. No daring adventures in your novels this morning?"

"Alas, my mother decided it was essential that we practice our embroidery…not that she needs to practice, with her perfect stitches."

"You do not enjoy embroidery then, Miss Lyttleton?"

She made the mistake of glancing up at him, and felt that all-too familiar whoosh in the pit of her stomach, which was always accompanied by all her thoughts disappearing from her head.

"Miss Lyttleton?"

She struggled to remember what the question had been, and what her answer ought to be, and for a few painful seconds they walked in silence, with him probably thinking she was the most empty-headed girl in London.

"I probably should not admit it," she said, when her mind finally decided to provide her mouth with words again, "but I find embroidery incredibly dull."

The earl laughed again. "It looks incredibly dull, so I cannot say I am surprised!"

"As a lady, of course, I am meant to enjoy it…"

"Just as I am supposed to enjoy shooting," the earl said. "And yet I find I have no desire to spend my leisure time surrounded by death and suffering. When the hunting season is upon us, I shall be derided for my lack of enthusiasm for the sport, I am sure."

Susannah focused on where she was walking, and did not look up at him, for she knew the effect that had on her. "It makes complete sense to me. We all have different tastes—I am never sure why society is so desperate for us all to be the same. How incredibly dull it would be if we were."

"It certainly would be," Lord Bourne agreed. "When I was traveling, I was amazed at just how different life can be in different countries, different cultures… There is no reason why we must all live in exactly the same way."

"And yet if you deviate from what is considered normal, you

are a social pariah—in London at least," Susannah said. "If you did not come by your wealth in the way everyone else did, or if your interests do not align with the rest of society…"

"Or if you prefer to travel the world and be called 'Colin' than being an earl, and the target of all the marriage-minded mamas of the ton…"

She *did* look up at him then. His face was serious, and his eyes determinedly focused on the path before him. She had not realized he felt so out of place in London. She knew he had not experienced London society in many years, but he always seemed so confident when he was out in public.

"Do you think you will be happier in the countryside, when the Season is over?"

He looked down at her and gave her a smile that made her trip over her own feet. He reached for her arm to steady her, but that only made her heart race. She hated how ridiculous she always appeared to be in front of him.

"Are you well?" he asked.

She nodded, and kept her eyes forward. *Yes, I'm simply besotted and overcome by your handsomeness.* "Yes, thank you."

"You mustn't think I'm unhappy, Miss Lyttleton. I certainly have no right to be. After speaking with my aunt this morning, I suppose I am just reflecting on how my life has changed. Please, ignore me."

"I wouldn't want to ignore you," Susannah said, before hurriedly adding, "Was your aunt well?"

"She…is older than when I last saw her, but she seems well," he said, but she felt as though he had wanted to say something else. Why had he remained out of the country for so very long— even once he had inherited the title? No one seemed to know, or at least they had not discussed it in her presence.

"You asked if I would be happier in the countryside," he said, as they reached the edge of the park. "And in truth, I have no idea. I am so used to moving around, to never truly settling, to having no one relying on me, that I am not sure whether I know how to live in a traditional way, as an earl."

"I suppose you could travel again, once you have reacquainted yourself with the estate?" Susannah suggested. He actually listened and seemed interested in what she had to say, when she managed to get the words out, and it was an unusual and pleasant experience.

He sighed. "Yes, I suppose so. But if I am to be a responsible earl… Well, one day I will need to wed, and have heirs to inherit. I cannot run away from it forever."

"I doubt I will ever see anywhere farther away than Newcastle," Susannah said with a sigh she couldn't stop.

"Your father has no wish to travel?"

She shook her head. "Now that he is accepted in the ballrooms, drawing rooms, and clubs he has always admired, he doesn't particularly like to leave London at all, let alone go farther than our home in Berkshire. And they are convinced that my best chance of finding a suitable husband is here."

CHAPTER NINE

S HE SPOKE OF marriage with as much enthusiasm as she did embroidery, and he could not help but ask, "Do you want to marry?"

She did not look at him as she replied. "Every young woman wants to marry, my lord."

"But do you?"

She glanced behind her, and he thought she was checking to see if her maid could overhear them before answering. "I…am not against marriage. In theory."

"But in practice?"

"In practice, no one has ever asked me, so the question is a pointless one." She flashed him a sad smile.

"And if they did?" He didn't know why he was pressing her on this. It was not really an appropriate conversation for acquaintances, and if he were truly courting her, he would surely have been rather disturbed to think she did not care for marriage.

And she was right; every young lady gave the impression that they wanted to wed, and soon. But surely that could not be true for all of them?

"I do not torture myself imagining such scenarios. But if I never marry, and can spend my days as I wish, I would not be devastated."

They reached the Lyttletons' carriage, and as Colin handed her in, he wondered if her parents knew that she had no real wish to wed. She did not seem to have any desire to run her own home or to have children—she just wanted to be free to live as she wished.

But would she really have any more freedom as an unwed spinster than she would as someone's wife?

⋙✦⋘

WHEN COLIN ENTERED the parlor, the room was rather quiet, with Miss Lyttleton and her mother embroidering.

Miss Lyttleton did not look like she was enjoying her morning's pursuits, and Colin wondered if he could somehow improve things for her.

"May I join you?" he asked, and both Miss and Mrs. Lyttleton looked up in surprise, having clearly not heard him enter the room. They both hurried to put down their embroidery to greet him, and he bowed his head in return. He still was not used to how formal everything had to be back in England. And it wasn't simply because he was now an earl; it was just the way things were done here. When he had traveled, however, most formalities had been dropped. He much preferred things that way.

"Of course, Lord Bourne. Please do. Why don't you take a seat next to Susannah? As you'll see, she is quite proficient with a needle and thread."

Susannah flashed him a brief smile, one which seemed to change her features altogether and made him unable to stop smiling back. Her sewing did indeed seem at a reasonable level, but it was clear—to him, anyway—that she took no pleasure in the task. She had told him as much when they had been out of earshot of her mother: how she longed to read instead of spending time on these feminine pursuits.

"It is a fine day we are having, is it not?" Colin said as he opened up the newspaper. He became very aware, suddenly, of how small the sofa was that he shared with Miss Lyttleton and how close they were. He watched her for a moment as she completed another row of stitches, leaving her mother to do the talking.

"Indeed, it is pleasantly mild. And I am pleased, for I must go to the modiste today, and London is so much more enjoyable in the sunshine than the rain."

"I daresay that could be said of most places, madam," Colin said with a smile. "But there is something about London that becomes particularly gray and dreary on a miserable day, I concur."

"We shall leave soon, Susannah," Mrs. Lyttleton said.

"Am I needed at the modiste, Mama?" Miss Lyttleton asked, looking even less enthused about the task than she did her embroidery. "For I have so recently had new dresses..."

"I need to choose fabrics for my own new gown," Mrs. Lyttleton said, putting down her embroidery and glancing over at Susannah. "But I do not think it's a sensible choice to leave you here..."

Her eyes darted momentarily to Colin, and he realized that his presence was making Mrs. Lyttleton worry about some possible impropriety. Of course, she did not know that the interest they had been showing each other was merely feigned, and that she did not need to worry about his presence.

But then, even if they had not been pretending to have formed an attachment, it would not be the done thing to leave a single young woman of marriageable age alone with an unwed young man.

He did not wish to be the reason Miss Lyttleton had to go on an outing she did not want. He thought he could go out himself and remove the obstacle...but then thought of a better solution.

"Perhaps, if Miss Lyttleton's maid could sit in the parlor with us, you might be willing to allow Miss Lyttleton to remain?" he asked, hoping that it would be Susannah's preference. "After all, it would give us some time to converse, away from the noise and bustle of the ballroom."

Mrs. Lyttleton did not look entirely convinced, but thankfully Miss Lyttleton jumped in to agree to the plan. "What a marvelous idea. You did promise me you would tell me more of your travels, and it is so much easier to do so in the peace of the drawing room—with my maid to chaperone, of course."

Mrs. Lyttleton still looked unsure, but she nodded anyway. "Well, I suppose. As long as Louise is present."

"Of course," Colin agreed. "Your home is the height of propriety, Mrs. Lyttleton."

Seeming mollified by the compliment, Mrs. Lyttleton finished her neat row of stitching before standing to make her departure.

Colin stood too, politely bowed his head, and then took his seat next to Miss Lyttleton once more.

For a few brief moments, they were alone, and Susannah flashed him a smile before putting her cross-stitch to one side.

"Thank you for saving me from a morning of sewing and a tedious trip to the modiste."

"You're very welcome," Colin replied. "And I am more than happy to discuss my travels—I'm afraid it's a topic I rarely tire of. But if you wish to read, I am also content to sit here and peruse the newspaper. I am happy to sit with you in chaperoned silence."

SUSANNAH DID NOT think that she had ever felt more seen, more understood, than she did in that moment. She was interested in his tales, but the fact that he understood her precious desire to simply read—that he had ensured she did not have to endure a dull morning with her mother and could instead follow her own passions—meant so much to her.

"You are a very understanding gentleman," she said, just as her maid walked into the room, taking a seat in the corner and beginning to work on a large pile of darning.

She did not say any more, now that they were not alone, but

she was beginning to see just how dangerous a man could be. For if one was so handsome that he took her breath away, and kind and thoughtful to boot, how on earth was she supposed to stop herself from falling head over heels in love with him?

She had always thought such behavior was only for silly girls, a notion they had been brought up to believe, and so, therefore, one they played up to. But she was beginning to realize that perhaps, where matters of the heart were concerned, one didn't have as much control as she had always imagined.

AFTER A PLEASANT half hour discussing his travels to Greece, Colin suggested that she read her book, and he reopened the newspaper that he had barely read upon first entering the parlor. There was nothing of any great interest in it, but he liked to keep abreast of what was going on wherever he was living. Every now and then, he found himself glancing up at Miss Lyttleton, who was so absorbed in her book that she barely seemed to be aware of her surroundings at all.

Her eyes darted across the page at great speed, and occasionally her mouth would move in a display of emotion that he could not quite read. Happiness for the characters? Or sadness for their plight? He could not quite tell, nor could he read the title from beneath her fingertips. He wanted to ask, but it seemed unfair to interrupt her when she was so absorbed.

She was, he thought as he watched her, the late morning sunshine streaming through the windows, rather prettier than he had first appreciated.

Why had the young men looking for wives not realized this? Along with a sizable dowry, it would surely make her an attractive marriage prospect. But then perhaps no one else had watched her like this, lost in emotions, so enthralled by the words before her that she was oblivious to the outside world. He felt rather honored to be sitting here with her, in the presence of the silently darning maid, with her guard so let down.

She glanced up and caught his eye, and he realized he had been staring at her for far too long. He hurriedly lowered his eyes to the newspaper, but was sure he felt his cheeks turning red. What a ridiculous reaction, he told himself. He had simply found her focus on the book interesting. There was nothing else to it.

CHAPTER TEN

ATTENDING BALLS WITH Lord Bourne was an entirely different experience from attending balls with just her mother and father. She was used to fading into the background, spending most of the evening looking on, rarely dancing, invisible to the sharp-eyed members of the ton.

But when she walked in with Lord Bourne, and when he showed her so much attention, she was no longer invisible.

All heads turned in their direction when they entered a ball-room, and the whispering began. Mostly, it was about Lord Bourne—where he'd been, who his father was, and why he had stayed out of the country for so long.

By the third ball, however, they seemed to have tired of discussing him endlessly, and the conversation turned to Susannah.

She hadn't meant to overhear it. In fact, she would rather not know what was being said about her. But the ladies gossiping were hardly discreet, and as she waited for refreshment, she could not help but hear the group of women nearby asking, "What on earth does he see in her?"

She wasn't so vain as to immediately assume the conversation was about her, but as it continued, there could be no doubt.

"No title, and her father worked for his money. That's how she's got such a large dowry."

"Perhaps the dowry is what the earl is interested in? He might be in desperate need of funds…"

Susannah held her glass far too tightly, knowing she ought to walk away, that nothing good could come of hearing such gossip—yet finding herself unable to.

"No. I don't think he's that desperately in need of money—not from what I hear. You know my brother spoke with him at White's last week. Money did not seem to be an issue. And I can hardly think he would align himself with a woman like that unless he was absolutely desperate."

The women chuckled unkindly, and Susannah felt tears pricking behind her eyes. She had thought she did not care what society thought of her, but she was realizing now that she had never truly heard it. She had been invisible, and that had felt like a burden—yet it was surely far better than knowing what people truly thought of you.

"She's just so plain. I mean, she's making a bit more effort with her dresses this Season, I presume to try to ensnare the earl. But an expensive dress and fine jewels cannot compensate for a lack of natural beauty. I'm sure Lord Bourne will see that, in time…"

Susannah was about to slip off to hide in the powder room and recover at least some semblance of control over her emotions when a male voice interrupted the ladies.

It was a familiar voice, one that made her heart and her mind trip.

"Lord Bourne can judge a person's looks and their character perfectly well without any help, thank you," Colin said in harsh, clipped tones. "You might want to think about how you are presenting your own characters, ladies, before you attack that of another."

And then he was gone, leaving Susannah speechless and frozen, not wanting a confrontation with the women, not wanting them to know that she had heard everything. And not wanting to find her faux beau any more attractive than she already did…

Lord Bourne had stood up for her. No one had ever done that

before. Oh, she was sure her parents loved her, but they had never publicly declared anything like that.

He hadn't denied that she was plain, of course. How could he? For that would be a lie. She knew she was plain and dull, and that was the reason she had never had an offer of marriage.

But beauty was not something one earned, learned, or deserved—it was just the luck of the draw. She had been born with brains and not beauty, and she rather thought she had the better deal than the girls who had been born with endless beauty but no brains.

And yet...

And yet it hurt to hear such things said aloud about her, even if she too had wondered if the ton would truly believe that the Earl of Bourne could be interested in a plain girl like Miss Susannah Lyttleton.

And now her heart felt full at the words he had spoken, at the fact that he had been quite willing to be rude to the ladies of the ton because they were being cruel about her.

She sought him out, her whole body flushed with warmth when their eyes met.

No, she did not think it was wholly believable that a man like the Earl of Bourne could fall for her.

But it was entirely possible that she could end up falling for the Earl of Bourne.

IRRITATION AT THE cruel words of the gossiping young ladies consumed him as Colin searched for Susannah. Why did they need to say such things? He hoped Susannah had not heard them, for the words would surely hurt. She was an interesting and intelligent young woman, and he preferred conversing with her to most other women of the ton. She might not have been classically pretty, but he no longer thought of her as plain. There was something about the sparkle in her eyes when she was interested in a topic, and the warm smile she gave him if he said or did something that made her happy that changed her unassuming appearance.

He did not think she had an unkind bone in her body, and he did not like the haughty attitudes of the women who looked down on her, who did not believe he could be interested in her unless he was in desperate need of her dowry.

He spotted her near the refreshment table—rather closer to where the gossiping women had been than he would have liked—and made a beeline for her. His hosts were dancing, and he had been avoiding the eyes of young women and their mamas who wanted him to ask them to dance. They had thankfully stopped stalking him around every ballroom now that most people believed he would soon be asking for Miss Lyttleton's hand in marriage, but it did not stop them hoping he would show some interest.

"May I have this dance, Miss Lyttleton?" he asked when he was close enough to speak to her. They had danced together on numerous occasions, but this time her cheeks flushed red, and she looked at the floor before meeting his gaze and nodding.

She took his offered hand without a word, and they cut through the crowds onto the dance floor. Colin was well aware that they were being watched, and by the gossips too, but that was what he wanted. The point of the ruse was for people to believe they were courting, and being seen together was essential for that. And if dancing together silenced the unkind critics, well, that was just a bonus.

He was surprised to find that, rather than dreading balls, he quite enjoyed them, now that the expectations on him had lessened. Conversation with Miss Lyttleton was always enjoyable, and every time he danced with her, he noticed something new about her that he hadn't before.

Sometimes she was chatty and sometimes, like in this dance, she seemed unable to find words. He still did not truly understand why shyness seemed to strike her at some times and not others, but he'd learned how to get her to speak to him.

"I started reading *Mansfield Park*," he said, and she immediately glanced up and met his eye.

"You did?"

"Well, you recommended it," he said with a smile.

"I know, but I did not think…" She trailed off. "Are you enjoying it?"

"I am. I must admit, there are far more layers to the story than I had expected. I think I will have to reread it more than once to truly glean every element of commentary Miss Austen is making."

And there it was—that smile that lit up her face, and made it impossible not to smile in return. "Indeed, I think you will. I have read it four times myself, and still think there is something new to be discovered."

"I can well imagine. And if you have any other recommendations for me to read next, I will gladly take them."

"I find it hard to choose my favorites from among all those I have read, but I am happy to suggest some options."

"You have read so many novels, you will have to start writing them or there will be none left for you to read!"

Her cheeks flushed pink and her eyes darted away from his.

"Do you write, as well as read?" he asked.

"No one would be interested in what I had to write," she said with a soft sigh.

He was struck with an urge to lift her chin so he could look into her brown eyes—but it was a ridiculous notion which he of course ignored. Instead he tutted and said, "With respect, that was not the question I asked."

She glanced up at him, faltering in the dance steps momentarily, and said softly, "I would like to write a novel. One day."

When the dance came to an end, they were still in deep conversation. Colin led Miss Lyttleton towards the refreshment table, and she seemed entirely unaware of the daggers glared at her from the unkind gossips who had been watching them.

He drew her arm in a little closer to his, and smiled with satisfaction as the gossips turned away in irritation.

CHAPTER ELEVEN

"DO YOU HAVE any plans for today, Lord Bourne?" Mrs. Lyttleton asked over breakfast. Miss Lyttleton sat opposite, seemingly very focused on the jam she spread on her toast. She did not seem to speak much in front of her parents, and yet when they spent time together without them, she was an interesting conversationalist.

"I need to speak with my lawyer, about some issues with my estate," Colin said. "And today seems the best day to do so. And then there is a musicale tonight, is that correct?"

"Yes, at Lady White's. Her daughters are exceptionally proficient in singing and playing, I think you will enjoy yourself." She shot her daughter a look. "And all are engaged to be wed, so I think this may be the last year we hear them all together."

Miss Lyttleton did not look up or acknowledge her mother's words, and Colin wondered if they had been heard before. It did seem that the Lyttletons saw nothing but faults in their daughter. He did not know what her singing voice was like, or whether she could play the pianoforte, but he did know that she was far more intelligent than most young women of his acquaintance, and more interesting too—and to him, that was more valuable than musical skills.

"And what do you plan to do with the day, Mrs. Lyttleton?" He glanced over at Susannah, hoping to draw her into the conversation. "Miss Lyttleton?"

She looked up, seeming rather surprised at being addressed, and smiled briefly before glancing at her mother.

"We have some calls to make this morning," Mrs. Lyttleton said. "And this afternoon, Susannah and I will meet with the housekeeper, and discuss the management of the house this month."

Miss Lyttleton frowned. "Do you need me to join you in that, Mama?"

Mrs. Lyttleton sighed. "You must learn how to run a household, Susannah. One day, when you are wed, you will need these skills. You cannot spend your life lost in a fictional world."

Susannah did not argue; she rarely seemed to. But he saw the flash of frustration cross her eyes before she returned to her breakfast. Was this preparation for running a house something Mrs. Lyttleton had always planned to do? Or was it because she was expecting a proposal of marriage, and soon—from him?

He hoped their ruse wasn't adding to Susannah's problems, rather than reducing them, as they had planned.

His lawyer had an office nearby, and as the weather was pleasant, Colin chose to walk there rather than take a horse. London was busy as always, and the fine weather had more people than usual out on the streets. He walked slowly, watching as people went about their daily lives. He was not particularly looking forward to this meeting. He knew he should have seen his lawyer sooner, and should have visited the estate, but he had wanted to ease himself back into society first.

And in truth, he didn't really wish to face the mess that he knew the estate was in. He was fairly sure there was still enough money for him to do a decent job of being earl, but his father had not kept things neat and tidy, financially speaking. There had been so many mistresses to be provided for, and so many properties used to house the women of his life, that Colin was sure it took a lot to maintain.

And with his man of business dead, and a new, young man in his place, he needed to make sure the earldom could still support everyone who relied on it.

Including all the women his father had dallied with, ultimately breaking his mother's heart.

No, the conversation with the lawyer was unlikely to be an enjoyable one, and so Colin took his time wandering to his office, putting off the moment for as long as he could.

⇻≫≪≺

SUSANNAH SAT AND sipped tea in Mrs. Selworthy's parlor, as her mother and Mrs. Selworthy gossiped about the Season. She found paying social calls rather dull, mainly because the topics of conversation were always to do with balls and young men and betrothals, and nothing of any substance.

And there were rarely any women of her own age when her mother took her calling, either. Her mother's friends did not seem to have twenty-five-year-old spinster daughters, and so there wasn't even anyone who might understand how she felt about the Season, and the endless attempts at finding a husband. They were either younger, and just coming out into society, excited about their prospects, or they were married off and visiting or hosting callers in their own homes, with their husbands.

"And how is your house guest?" Mrs. Selworthy asked, glancing at Susannah with a grin. "I hear he has shown you a special interest, Susannah dear."

Susannah felt blood rushing to her cheeks at the attention, and at the thought of Lord Bourne.

She did not know how to respond to Mrs. Selworthy's comments and was relieved when her mother jumped in with an answer.

"Lord Bourne is a very charming young man," she said, reaching for her cup of tea. "He is a perfect gentleman, and yes, he has shown Susannah some favor this Season."

"How intriguing," Mrs. Selworthy said, with a glance over at Susannah. "How fortunate you are that he is staying in your home. He is a very handsome and eligible young man."

Mrs. Selworthy had three daughters, all of whom were wed, so Susannah did not understand why she needed to sound quite so irritated that Lord Bourne might have shown an interest in her. Of course, it was not real—but she had to make sure people believed it was. For Lord Bourne's sake, even if it did not matter so much to her.

"He is a very well-brought-up young man, and we are very pleased to host him for the Season," Mama said, either ignoring the slight or choosing not to respond to it.

"Well, I am glad to hear so. He certainly brings a bit of excitement to the Season. It can get dreadfully dull, with the same faces being around year after year."

Susannah felt her cheeks flaming red and looked down into her tea. She was one of those faces who had been there for years. One of the boring ones. One of the ones who would be there until she was allowed to accept defeat and stop attending so many events in the hopes of securing a husband.

"And I'm glad to hear he's a gentleman, too," Mrs. Selworthy said. "For I'm sure you've heard all about his father, and his…proclivities."

Susannah's head snapped up. She knew nothing of the former Lord Bourne, nor to what proclivities Mrs. Selworthy might be referring.

"Well, one hears rumors…" Mama said delicately. "But one cannot judge the son for the sins of the father."

"No, of course not," Mrs. Selworthy agreed, and then the conversation returned to gossip in which Susannah had little interest. She felt rather irritated that the one interesting topic her mother and Mrs. Selworthy discussed had been cut off so quickly. Not because she was keen to gossip, but because she found she was interested in knowing as much about Lord Bourne as she could.

As they walked briskly back towards home, Susannah's intrigue got the better of her, and she decided to broach the topic with her mother.

"What did Mrs. Selworthy mean, Mama, when she mentioned Lord Bourne's father?"

Mama was silent for a moment, and Susannah thought that she had not heard the question—or was going to pretend she had not, in any case.

"It was just gossip, Susannah. And not suitable for your ears. Mrs. Selworthy should have known better."

Now she was really intrigued. She waited another moment before trying with a different tact.

"I just thought, since Lord Bourne does seem to have shown an interest in me, that I should be prepared in case anyone challenges me on such gossip."

Her mother glanced at her, then turned her attention back to the pavement, gritting her teeth. "I do not want to hear it spoken of again, do you understand?"

She shouldn't have been surprised her mother would tell her nothing. She resisted sighing as she nodded. "Yes, Mama."

"And you mustn't mention it to the earl. It would be highly inappropriate, and you might offend him."

"I understand," Susannah said, struggling not to show how eager she was to learn such an interesting piece of information about the man who was staying with them.

"Lord Bourne… that is, the previous Lord Bourne…had a rather unfortunate reputation. He…" It seemed her mother was having trouble putting the gossip into words, and Susannah waited impatiently for her to finish.

"He was not faithful in his marriage…which, of course, is not altogether uncommon. But he had such an interest in women that it was enough to be remarked upon."

"So he had…a mistress?"

Mama tutted. "This is not an appropriate topic of conversation. But yes, I believe he had many mistresses—and that it broke his wife's heart to know it. Now, I do not want to hear any more about it, understood? Lord Bourne is not the same man as father, and this does not change anything. But you will be prepared now if anyone chooses to be so indelicate as to gossip about it in front of you."

CHAPTER TWELVE

"Ah, it's a pleasure to see you, Lord Bourne," Colin's lawyer said when Colin eventually arrived at his office. He was a small man with a powdered wig and eyes that looked a little too small for his face. Colin had never met him before, though they had exchanged letters.

"Thank you for seeing me, Mr. Linden," Colin said as the little man bustled about. He really did not want to be there, but that was no excuse to be anything less than polite. It wasn't Mr. Linden's fault, after all, that his father had made such a mess of the estate.

"Please, take a seat. I have all the paperwork ready for us to look at. Can I get you something to drink? Tea? Something a little stronger?"

"It's a little early in the day for me," Colin said, as it was not even noon. "But I'll take some tea, thank you."

The desk was covered in pieces of parchment, and Colin took a deep breath before sitting down. He found it hard to face anything that reminded him of how his father had treated his mother, of how brokenhearted she had been, and of how things had never been put right between them before her death.

He understood that many husbands, especially those in the upper classes, were not faithful to their wives...but his father could have been a little less prolific—or more discreet, in any case. His mother shouldn't have needed to be so aware of his behavior, to hear the gossip, as Colin was sure she had.

"Now," Mr. Linden said, rubbing his hands together before sitting down, "since you have been away for so long, there is quite a lot I need to get you up to speed on. The estate still has a decent fortune, and old Mr. Wicks—may he rest in peace—kept things running very smoothly. I have not met the new man—"

"Mr. Steadman," Colin supplied. "I have not met him either. I gather he is eager, but young and inexperienced."

"And I presume you intend to return to your estate once the Season is over?"

Colin nodded. He didn't particularly wish to return to the house that was full of his childhood memories, but he knew that he had to.

"That is my intention, yes. But I want to make sure everything is in order. So please, Mr. Linden, tell me what the most pressing concerns are."

Mr. Linden proceeded to give him a thorough rundown of every single property that his father had allowed a mistress to use, and every single piece of jewelry that had left the family coffers to adorn the necks of his ladies.

"The only jewels left are those your mother bequeathed to you, presumably for your future wife: a wedding ring, a ruby brooch, and a diamond necklace. I do not think any are worth great sums, although there is no need for you to sell them. But should you wish to replenish the family jewels—perhaps before taking a wife—I thought you ought to be aware of the situation."

Colin nodded curtly. It was one thing to have known of his father's behavior, but another altogether to be discussing the particulars of it in broad daylight with his lawyer.

"And the estate can continue to support all of these outgoings without bankrupting it?"

Mr. Linden nodded. "Yes, for the time being. For your lifetime, in fact. But the problem will arise, and indeed has arisen, when the occupants of the houses pass on. If their children or other relatives then decide that they ought to live there, even though the houses are still owned by the Bourne estate—well, it can become quite complicated."

"I see. So some of these ladies have already…passed on?"

Mr. Linden referred to his notes. "Three have, my lord. One handed the estate back before her death so that there could be no confusion. But the other two have children or relatives living in the homes even now that they are gone. They pay no rent, and my concern is that this could become a burden that not only follows you for your entire life but also your children and your children's children. I fear some formal documentation must be drawn up to outline how far the gift your father gave will continue."

"That seems sensible," Colin said, not wishing for any children he might have to be burdened because of the sins of their grandfather. At the same time, he did not wish to see anyone on the streets; he was well aware that his father had been a rich and powerful man, and the women who had fallen into bed with him were not necessarily doing so to be cruel to his mother. But he also would not see his estate suffer or money frittered away because of his father's poor decisions that could be put to better use.

He left the lawyer's office after almost two hours, feeling like he at least knew the state of his finances, even if it was all rather messy. So many homes were occupied by women he'd never met, and never had or would have any wish to meet. He was happy to leave the paperwork in his lawyer's hands, but he knew he couldn't keep his head in the sand now that he was home. It was his responsibility to make sure the estate could support those it needed to, and that it was in good shape to pass down to his heir one day—and he wasn't going to abandon his responsibilities any longer.

Perhaps waiting until the end of the Season to return to his estate was too long, he thought as he wandered back to the Lyttletons' townhouse. He was enjoying the Season, and attending events with Miss Lyttleton, far more than he had expected—but was he simply putting off his obligations?

CHAPTER THIRTEEN

T HE GLASS RATTLED in the windowpanes as Susannah tried in vain to sleep.

It had rained all day, which had not displeased her, since it gave her a good excuse to stay in and read. But now the rain had turned into a storm, and she was frustrated that the noise was stopping her from falling asleep.

With a sigh, she got up and wrapped herself in her night rail. Her fire had long since burned out, and the room was chilly. She padded over to the window and drew back the curtains enough to look out onto the deserted streets. Occasionally, the clouds scudded across the sky, allowing a sliver of moonlight to illuminate the street below.

It was rather eerie to see the usually bustling London so quiet, being battered by the rain and wind. She shivered, pleased that she did not need to go out in it.

She could not lie in bed for hours, desperately trying to sleep. It felt like a futile exercise, and one in which she had no wish to participate. If she was going to be awake, she might as well be reading. Lighting a candle, she pulled her latest tome from her bedside table and got back under the covers, holding the candle close so she could read the words.

When she had been younger, her mother had caught her more than once reading by candlelight and had scolded her—not just for staying up past her bedtime, but because she said that squinting in the darkness would ruin her eyesight and cause her to have unsightly lines around her eyes. Lines that no man would find attractive.

And she supposed that her mother had been right. But what was the point in ceasing night-time reading now? Everyone knew she was plain, and if anyone did propose marriage, it would only be for her dowry. She wasn't going to give up one of her greatest pleasures for that.

She was rather disappointed to find that she only had a handful of pages left in the novel, and they were soon read. If anything, she felt more wide awake than before, and worse, now she was desperate to start a new book.

But that would involve venturing to the library in the dead of night…

She hadn't exactly been forbidden from doing so, but she was well aware that her mother would disapprove—especially now that they had the Earl of Bourne staying with them.

As she debated what to do, her thoughts lingered on Lord Bourne. She knew what she was feeling for him was unwise. That she shouldn't watch him across the table at supper or look forward to their dances together.

She couldn't help it. She had never felt this way before. And if she was well aware that his feelings were entirely feigned, who was she hurting?

At the end of the Season, he would return to his estate, they would make some excuse as to why their courtship had ended, and she would go back to living her regular life.

But for now… But for now, surely she could enjoy feeling this way, something she had never felt before?

Having decided that sitting around and thinking about Lord Bourne was not a sensible use of a stormy, sleepless night, Susannah put thoughts of Mother's displeasure aside, picked up her candle, and made her way to the library.

The corridor was dark and deserted, with only the shadows her flickering candle produced keeping her company. Occasionally, there was a creak or a bang that made her jump, but she knew it was just the wind battering the house.

She was relieved when she reached the door to the library, partly because it was unpleasant to walk through the house at this time of night, and partly because she'd been afraid she'd be spotted by her mother or father—or perhaps worse, run into Lord Bourne in a state of undress.

But when she pushed open the library door, she was surprised to find that it was not empty and dark. No, there was a fire roaring in the grate, and a familiar figure sat in the armchair before it.

→》》X《《←

WHEN THE LIBRARY door creaked open, Colin assumed it was just a draft from the storm raging outside. He finished the line he was reading, then looked up—and was rather shocked to see Miss Lyttleton in the doorway, carrying a candle, barefoot and with her hair flowing down her back, unrestrained.

It did not escape his notice that she was wrapped in a night rail that clung to her curves and showed far more of her legs than any outfit he had ever seen her in. He swallowed involuntarily and felt his cheeks warm. Belatedly, he stood up and bowed his head to her—a gesture that felt rather formal, considering the situation.

"Good evening, Miss Lyttleton," he said, hoping his voice did not betray the surprising surge of lust that had shot through him at the sight of her.

"Good...good evening," she said, her voice shaking a little. Was she scared of him? Or just as surprised to see him as he had been to see her?

"I—I could not sleep. And I finished my book...so I thought I would come and fetch another," she said in response to his unasked question.

"The storm is rather loud, isn't it? I will leave you in peace to select your book." He sat back down and opened his book, just so he'd have something to stare at instead of the woman before him. Except he couldn't seem to make himself look at anything but her.

She shook her head. "There is no need for you to leave, Lord Bourne." Her eyes darted to the fire and to his half-drunk glass of whiskey on the table. "I will only be a moment, and then you can continue in peace."

Colin shook his head. "It is your home, Miss Lyttleton. I would not dream of imposing in such a way."

In truth, his chivalry was not entirely due to it being her home, but also because the thoughts in his head were not appropriate to be having at this time of night around an unmarried but marriageable young woman dressed in only her night clothes. While he was still clothed, he had long since divested himself of his cravat, removed his boots, and untucked his shirt. And although he had thought she was prettier than the rumors gave her credit for, he had never felt like this before.

Like how he wanted to see how she would react if he crossed the room and kissed her. How he wanted to cup the small, round breasts he could see outlined through her night clothes, and how he thought he could tell exactly where her nipples were. How he imagined they would be the same color as her pink lips, and how he longed to hear her lose control as he introduced her to pleasures of which she surely had no knowledge.

No, these were not thoughts he ought to be having about the woman he was pretending to court. These were thoughts to have about courtesans, opera singers, or widowed ladies seeking a night of passion. Not innocent young women who were expecting to make a good match—and certainly not ones in whose homes he was a guest.

"Please, I would feel terrible if your evening was disturbed because of my late-night wanderings. And I would appreciate it if you did not mention my appearance here to my mother. She would not approve."

She flashed him one of those smiles that made him feel even more attracted to her, and he thought her mother probably had very good reasons for not approving. If she had any notion her daughter might inspire such feelings in the young man staying with them, then she was entirely justified in her strictness.

And yet, he could not seem to say "no" to her. "Very well," he murmured, wishing she would choose her book quickly—just as much as he wished she wouldn't leave.

CHAPTER FOURTEEN

H E WAS LOOKING at her in a way she did not understand, and she could only think he was appalled at her wandering the hallways in her night clothes. She was mortified beyond belief, but still—she was even more desirous of a new book to read, so she hurried to the shelf in the library where her favorite novels were kept, taking her candle with her, for the light from the fire did not fully illuminate their titles.

She tried to be quick, knowing it was not appropriate for her to be in the library with him like this, but she found it hard to focus, knowing he was right there, reading his book and sipping his whiskey behind her.

Having made her selection—a book of Miss Austen's, which she had already read but hoped would provide comfort on this long, dark, and embarrassing night—she turned around to find the Earl of Bourne was not reading his book. Instead, he sat simply watching her.

A delicious thrill surged through her body, and for a moment, they simply watched one another, not speaking, the sound of the fire crackling in the grate and the wind and rain outside the only interruptions.

"I—" She wasn't sure what she had been about to say. Perhaps that she ought to return to her room, or maybe a comment on the storm. But before she could, there was a flash of lightning and a crack of thunder, and she jumped, sending her candle skittering across the floor. She squeaked in shock, and Lord Bourne jumped up and rushed over, ensuring the candle at her feet was extinguished before reaching out to touch her arm.

"Are you hurt?" he asked, but she could not answer. The feeling of his warm fingertips against her bare skin sent any words in her mind far, far away. His touch was much more powerful than his looks—and she had been silenced by them before.

"I—" Again, she had no idea what the end of the sentence would be, and she never got to find out. She looked up at him, and the next thing she knew, he was leaning toward her, his lips crashing against hers, the breath knocked out of her, her heart racing.

If she had known kissing felt like this, she thought she might have been more concerned about the fact that she was heading toward life as a spinster without ever having experienced it.

But how could she have known?

And perhaps kissing wasn't always like this. Perhaps this was specific to Colin.

His hand moved to her loose hair as he pulled her closer to his body. She could feel the heat of him through the thin layer she wore, and the strength of his muscles pressed against her. It was scandalous. It was delicious. It was like nothing she had ever imagined.

She kissed him back just as enthusiastically, even if she wasn't sure what she was doing. Their tongues met, and a spark of something she thought must be desire shot through her, making her lean into him more, making her want more...

If this was wrong, then why did it feel so good?

All of the unspoken desire she had been feeling since Colin had arrived at their home was poured into that kiss. It was hard to believe that this man—this handsome, mysterious, kind man—was kissing her. It was the last thing she'd expected on that stormy night when she had ventured to the library in search of a book to pass the hours when she could not sleep.

Feeling rather bold, she pressed her hand against his chest, feeling the warmth of his skin through the thin shirt he wore. He held her closer, and she went willingly, not wanting to be parted from him, not wanting this moment to end.

And yet, of course, it had to.

Another flash of lightning, so similar to the one that had set this in motion, lit up the library—and both of them froze in shock. Then Susannah slowly pulled away and looked up at the disheveled earl. His eyes were sparkling in the firelight, and his lips were swollen and red. She could only imagine what she looked like.

And then she gasped. She was wearing only her night rail and was alone with a gentleman who had just kissed her so thoroughly that she wasn't sure she could even walk.

And yet walk she must. Running, even better. She was sure that at any moment, he would realize what a mistake he had made. He would apologize; he would be polite, but it would be clear in his eyes that he regretted such a foolish action.

Or he might judge her for having given in so willingly, for not once protesting that she should not be kissing him, that they should not even be alone together.

And she didn't want to see any of that on his face, so she turned on her heel and fled the room—not remembering to take the book she had gone to fetch and without her candle to light her way through the dark and windy corridor.

FOR A FEW moments after Miss Lyttleton had fled, Colin stood in shock, trying to get his head around what had just happened.

One minute he had been reading alone in the library. The next, he was faced with the tantalizing vision of Miss Lyttleton in her nightclothes. And then…and *then* he had kissed her.

There was no denying it. She had seemingly been a willing participant, but he was sure he had instigated it.

And he had not wanted it to end. In fact, he rather thought he might well have gone much further than kissing if the lightning had not interrupted them.

Had she not run away.

When he felt able to walk, he returned to the wingback armchair by the fireplace and swiftly downed his glass of whiskey. He was rather surprised to find how much the incident had shaken him. It wasn't as though he had never kissed a woman before. But he had never kissed a lady who might well be expecting marriage. He had never been so surprised by the desire this particular lady made him feel. And he had never come so close to compromising an innocent young woman.

He had lost his head. Spending so much time with her and pretending to court her had clearly interfered with his thoughts. The logical, well-brought-up Colin would never have done such a thing. This version of himself seemed to lose all control.

Because of her.

Because of a woman whom everyone thought plain, but who Colin was beginning to think was anything but.

He had obviously offended her beyond words. Now, he watched the flames flicker in the grate, looking like people dancing, and shuddered at the thought of her running from the room because of his impropriety.

And what on earth was he to do about it? Go after her and apologize? He could not do that. She would be back in her bedchamber, and that was somewhere he definitely did not belong.

And if he tried to discuss it with her, would he simply embarrass her further? Draw attention to something she would rather forget?

They had a plan—and, he thought, he had probably ruined it. There was an understanding between them that there was to be a false understanding, and yet here he was, kissing her. Losing himself in her. Wanting so much more…

Perhaps, to make things easier, he should just pretend the kiss had never happened. Carry on as though nothing between them had changed, as though it were just a pleasant dream from which he had unfortunately been awakened.

Yes, he decided. That would be the best—or at least, the easiest—course of action. He hoped.

⫸⫷

SUSANNAH MADE IT back to her room quicker than she had thought possible, even without any light to guide her. She shut the door behind her, wincing when it banged and hoping the noise could not be heard over the storm, and rushed to climb into bed, as though she could pretend nothing had happened and she had never left her room.

Her heart was racing and she couldn't catch her breath.

Had that really just happened? Had she just kissed the Earl of Bourne, with reckless abandon, in the library, wearing only her nightclothes?

If anyone found out, it would be the scandal of the Season.

The memory of the kiss sent heat flooding through her body, and did nothing to help her heart stop racing.

Her first ever kiss. And with a man as desirable as the Earl of Bourne.

She had no idea why he had kissed her, why he had pulled her close, what had possessed him. She knew exactly why she had kissed him back; because she wanted to. Because she had feelings for him that extended beyond friendship, beyond the fake courtship they were showing to the world. Because he was handsome and funny and kind and she had never been kissed before…

Do not let your heart run away with your head, she told herself as the storm continued to rage outside. *It undoubtedly meant nothing more to him. And remember, his father was a rake. Perhaps he is not so different…*

But when she finally fell asleep, she could not help but dream of a repeat occurrence, and of finding out what would have happened if that sudden flash of lightning had not caused them to jump apart.

CHAPTER FIFTEEN

T HE NEXT MORNING, Susannah woke early, in spite of her late night. She rang the bell for her maid to help her dress, but she could not focus on the conversation that young Louise was making. All she could think about was that kiss. The way Lord Bourne's blue eyes had sparkled in the firelight. The way her heart had swooped and her thoughts had become illogical when his lips had pressed against hers.

And now she would have to see him over breakfast. See him…and pretend nothing had happened. For even if he wanted to discuss the incident, which she presumed he would not, her parents would be present, and so they could not acknowledge that anything was any different between them at all.

And then the following night they were to attend a ball together, and she would have to pretend they were courting, but also pretend to him that her thoughts weren't consumed by that kiss. Because his certainly wouldn't be. He was a man, for a start—and she had always heard that men did not feel the same way about a kiss as women did. Not that she'd had any experience of how wonderful a kiss could be, before… But she had overheard plenty of gossip, from her position on the edge of society and of the dance floor.

"Will there be anything else, Miss Lyttleton?" Louise asked as she finished tying a ribbon in the plait down Susannah's back.

"No, thank you Louise." As her maid tidied away the pins and the hairbrush, Susannah studied her face in the mirror. Her hair and eyes were the most boring shade of brown, and her nose always seemed to be too small, and her eyes a little too wide. Today, her cheeks were pink, as were her lips, and thinking about her lips only caused her to blush more.

Did she look different after the kiss? Would anyone be able to tell?

With nerves fluttering in her stomach, she left her room and made her way downstairs. She could hear from the clatter of dishes and the sound of voices that the dining room was not empty, and when she pushed the door open, she found she was the last to arrive.

"Good morning," she said softly, avoiding looking at Lord Bourne, who had stood as soon as she had arrived.

"Good morning, Miss Lyttleton." His voice was deep and calm.

She barely paid attention to her parents' greetings as she slid into her seat, tripping over the chair leg as she did so.

"Be careful, Susannah!" her mother admonished with a tut.

"Sorry." If her cheeks had been pink before, they were surely positively scarlet by now. She had tried to enter without drawing attention to herself, but had done the complete opposite.

"The storm seems to have blown itself out, thankfully," Papa said. "Such a lot of noise last night. I thought the roof might come down!"

Susannah looked up and caught the earl's eye, and was rather pleased to see him blushing and looking awkwardly away, too. It was the only sign that their kiss had not been completely in her mind.

"I hope it didn't keep you awake, Lord Bourne," Mama said. "Especially with your room being next to that large tree."

Lord Bourne coughed, and Susannah looked down at her empty plate as he replied, not trusting her expression not to give something away.

"It did keep me awake...for a while. The tree wasn't a problem though, don't worry."

She wondered how long he had spent in the library, once she had run off. Was that why he had not heard the branches of the tree being blown around in the wind?

"You look tired, Susannah," Mama said in a disapproving voice.

"The storm kept me awake," she said quickly.

"And your cheeks are red. I hope you aren't sickening for anything—you know how important the Merriweather Ball tomorrow night is."

"I'm well, Mama," Susannah reassured her—although she wasn't sure how it would have been her fault if she had been sick and missed the ball. She would hardly have done it on purpose. And yet anything she seemed to do was always wrong, in her mother's eyes.

"You will be joining us, will you not, Lord Bourne?"

He hesitated for long enough that Susannah glanced up at him, wondering if the kiss had made him not want to attend, or not want to pretend to be courting her.

"It's one of the biggest events of the Season," Papa said. "I believe your aunt may also be in attendance. She usually is."

Lord Bourne nodded. "I really ought to see her soon. Yes, I shall join you—although I am not sure if I can now remain for the entirety of the Season."

CHAPTER SIXTEEN

SUSANNAH SAW COLIN conversing with an elderly woman on the other side of the ballroom. There was a distinct resemblance between the two—the same nose and the same mouth. She felt sure this was Colin's aunt, who knew her parents, although she had never met her in person.

She wondered if she ought to go over and make conversation, and introduce herself—for even though the connection between her and the earl was fake, no one else knew that.

Before she could make her way through the crush of people surrounding the dance floor, the earl had led his aunt from the room, and Susannah was unsure whether or not to follow.

She had found herself feeling increasingly unsure after that kiss.

Her first kiss.

It had been so unexpected, so magical, so mind-blowing…and then she had run off, and now she had no idea how to act around the earl anymore. She hadn't really known how to act around him before, with his good looks and the way he made her heart race.

She still didn't really understand why he had kissed her. She presumed the ambiance of the moment, with the fire in the grate and the storm raging outside, had clouded his senses. For there was certainly no way she could inspire within him the same heart-stopping feelings he inspired within her.

He seemed to be pretending like the kiss had never happened, and so she was doing the same. Her parents would surely be furious if they found out about the incident—or they would be thrilled and use it to push the two into marriage.

And while the thought of marrying the earl was an attractive one—far more attractive than she had ever considered marriage to be before—she was not going to force the man to wed her because of a moment of weakness and a single kiss in the library.

Even if she thought that the kiss would play on her mind until her dying breath.

Deciding to take them some refreshment, Susannah collected two glasses of ratafia and then headed toward the exit they had taken into the hallway. She presumed his aunt wished to sit or take some air, for the ballroom was rather stuffy. When there was no sight of them in the corridor, she glanced out of the large main doors, which had been left open to allow some air to flow through.

And that was when she saw them—his aunt seated on a stone bench a little way from the door, Colin standing next to her.

And that was when she heard them.

"You must understand my concern, Colin. I'm sure she is a sweet girl, but other than a dowry—which you are not in need of—she would bring nothing to your marriage. No title, no looks, no contacts in society. And as for heirs—well, her mother only produced one daughter, so she might not be successful there, either."

Realizing she was the topic of the conversation, Susannah shrank back into the shadows, holding the two glasses as best she could and trying not to make a noise.

She saw Colin put his hand to his head and let out an exasperated sigh. "Really, Aunt, you mustn't—"

"I mean no ill toward the girl, but she must be aware of what society expects from you. At the end of the Season, when you return to your estate, there will be much for you to do—and then it will be time to find a wife. An *appropriate* wife. Do you understand?"

Once again, Colin sighed. "I understand what you are saying, Aunt. Rest assured, I have no plans whatsoever to marry Miss Lyttleton."

Susannah bit her bottom lip to stop herself from making a sound. Of course, this was not news. And yet it hurt, all the same. After that kiss… Oh, who was she kidding? Before the kiss. Her feelings had not remained false. But it seemed that his had. She knew she shouldn't have been surprised by it, or hurt by it…but she was.

She knew she ought to return to the ballroom, to pretend she had heard nothing, that her heart was not aching, but she could not tear herself away.

"You're not?" his aunt asked, surprise in her voice. "But surely you are aware of the impression—"

Colin glanced around, seemingly checking to make sure no one was listening, and Susannah stepped further back so she could still hear him but could not see him and did not risk him seeing her.

"I am aware of the impression I am giving, Aunt. As is Miss Lyttleton. Do not concern yourself."

"I see. But—" It seemed that his aunt was keen to ask further questions, but Colin cut her off.

"Our absence will be noted, Aunt," he said. "Please allow me to escort you back into the ballroom."

Susannah hurried back inside so quickly that she very nearly tripped and fell on her face, only catching herself in the nick of time. The contents of the two glasses sloshed around, spilling on the floor, and she handed them to a bemused-looking footman before rushing to the powder room.

She did not want Colin to see her upset. Or anyone else, for that matter. She did not want to explain why she was hurting. That she was a foolish girl who had fallen for a lie. A lie she had told herself. A lie that she had known full well would never become truth.

And yet…there had been moments where she had almost

believed that this thing between them was real. When he had stood up for her, when he had gone out of his way to make her happy, when he had kissed her.

He had no plans to marry her. Of course, he didn't. He was the handsome and enigmatic Earl of Bourne, who could have any woman he chose.

And she was the plain, on-the-shelf spinster—the wallflower Miss Lyttleton with a large dowry and no family connections.

And as he had told his aunt: she was well aware that none of this was real.

So how on earth had she let herself begin to believe it?

CHAPTER SEVENTEEN

Wᴇɴ ʜᴇ ʀᴇᴛᴜʀɴᴇᴅ to the ballroom after the rather frustrating conversation with his aunt, in which he had been forced to tell her that his relationship with Miss Lyttleton was not going to end in marriage, he tried to find Susannah. She often disappeared into the background at events like these, and yet he normally never struggled to locate her. He wondered, really, how she had been overlooked for so many years when she had so many qualities to recommend her.

But on this occasion, he could not find her. She was not in any of the places she usually frequented when avoiding her parents at a ball, and when he found her parents, they also had no idea of her whereabouts—not that he was particularly surprised by that. They did seem very quick to ignore her.

"Lord Bourne, what a pleasure to see you," a deep yet feminine voice said, and he turned to find Lady Linley and her three daughters. He had met them at one of the first balls of the Season, but had managed to avoid them more successfully after making the agreement with Miss Lyttleton in Vauxhall Gardens. However, now he found himself alone and surrounded by the four rather intimidating ladies, each dressed in a different jewel tone, and waving around matching fans.

He bowed his head. "And it's a pleasure to see you, Lady Linley."

"I presume you remember my daughters?" she said, waving

her hand to indicate the three young ladies beside her, all of whom were smiling in his direction. "Lady Emerald, Lady Jade, and Lady Ruby."

Once again he bowed his head in greeting, trying to think how he could extricate himself from the situation. He had no desire to have to offer dances to all three girls, and quite possibly their mother as well. They weren't unattractive, but they did not seem to share one sensible thought between them, and it would be a painfully silent dance which he would rather avoid.

It was at that moment that he saw Miss Lyttleton re-enter the room, and make a beeline for her parents. Although Lady Linley was speaking, Colin found his attention captured by the young lady he was pretending to court. The conversation between them looked fraught; Mrs. Lyttleton's face was scrunched up in irritation, and Miss Lyttleton kept looking at the floor.

"Have you been enjoying the dancing this evening, Lord Bourne?" Lady Linley asked, and Colin forced his attention back to the ladies.

"I—the musicians are very talented," he answered, hoping he could escape the conversation without being forced to ask them to dance out of politeness.

"They certainly are," Lady Linley continued, undeterred. "The Merriweathers always put on an incredible ball. But we are sadly lacking gentlemen tonight. Can you believe my daughters have each only danced twice so far this evening?"

He opened his mouth to reply, feeling the trap closing in around him, but before he could respond, Mr. Lyttleton hurried over.

"My apologies for interrupting," he said, with a nod to Lady Linley and her daughters. "I'm afraid Susannah is feeling unwell, and so we must return home. We can of course send the carriage back for you..."

Colin immediately glanced over to where he had last seen Susannah with her parents, but she was already gone. He hoped she did not feel too ill. Her mother had commented on her looking tired and rosy-cheeked the previous day, but he had put that down to their unexpected liaison, and not illness. But perhaps he had been wrong.

"Oh, I could not inconvenience you in that way," he said, taking the opportunity while he could. "Lady Linley, ladies, it has been a pleasure, as always. Good evening."

And then he walked away with Mr. Lyttleton, knowing that he had been rude, but very pleased to have escaped the three—or possibly even four—dull dances he had been about to be trapped into.

The carriage was awaiting them outside, with the ladies already in it, and when Colin stepped in, he immediately turned to look at Miss Lyttleton. She looked pale this evening, although he did not remember thinking so when they had left the house.

In fact, he had found himself thinking how pretty she looked in the shade of ice blue that she was wearing...but that wasn't a notion he thought he ought to dwell on.

"I am sorry to hear you are unwell, Miss Lyttleton," he said, as Mr. Lyttleton sat next to him on the bench and the door closed.

"We are sorry to cut your evening short, Lord Bourne," Mrs. Lyttleton said, seemingly with no concern at all for her daughter's wellbeing.

"It is just a headache," Miss Lyttleton murmured, glancing at him and then looking away. He swore he saw hurt in her eyes, and hoped she was not in too much pain.

"I've told you, you read too much. That won't be helping the pain in your head."

"I'm sorry, Mama," she said, her voice full of sorrow.

When they returned home, Colin was keen to speak with her, to check that she wasn't too unwell, but she hurried off to bed before he had the chance.

Since agreeing to pretend to court, they had conversed and laughed together fairly easily, and he found he missed it. He only hoped she would feel better the following day, and things would go back to the way they had been.

At the back of his mind, he worried that she was behaving differently because of their kiss. But she had seemed fine at the beginning of the evening. She had danced with him, and they had laughed at the behavior of the clearly very inebriated couple dancing next to them.

So it must be the headache causing her distance—for he could think of nothing that had changed over the course of the evening.

❧⟫⟫⟫✳⟪⟪⟪❧

COLIN BARELY SAW Miss Lyttleton for three days after the ball, and he began to worry that she was sicker than her parents were letting on.

He asked after her health every day, but he did not feel he could do more than that. He was tempted to knock on her bedchamber door to check that she was all right...but he knew it would not be appropriate. He did not want to make her life more difficult.

When she finally came down for breakfast on the fourth day, her eyes looked a little puffy and her face pale, but she did not seem particularly weak, for which he was grateful.

"I am pleased you are feeling better," Colin said. He had been surprised at how much he had missed her company in the few days she had been secluded away. Mr. and Mrs. Lyttleton were always pleasant to him, but they were not nearly as interesting to converse with as Miss Lyttleton. He enjoyed trying to make her laugh, seeing her eyes light up, and watching how a smile could change her whole face.

And if he ever thought about kissing those lips... Well, he would certainly keep that to himself. But it was not an unenjoyable sensation to recall the kiss he had shared with the young lady before him.

"Thank you, Lord Bourne." She did not meet his eyes, and he

wondered again whether he had offended her when he had kissed her. Well, of course, he had. She was a well-brought-up young lady, and he was supposed to be a gentleman. Except...except he was sure that she had kissed him back with just as much enthusiasm. He didn't think he could have imagined that sort of passion.

"It's a lovely day, by the looks of it. Perhaps we could promenade this afternoon?" he suggested.

"I am not sure if I feel—" Miss Lyttleton began.

"I think it's a splendid idea," Mrs. Lyttleton said, overruling her daughter. "Some fresh air, a little sunshine—just what you need after feeling ill in your room these past days."

"I—"

Whatever Susannah had been about to say was silenced by a sharp look from her mother. Colin felt rather guilty. He could tell she did not particularly wish to promenade, and he knew he ought to find a way to let her off the hook. But he was also feeling rather desperate to have a moment when he could speak to her, to check that she was well, and to make sure she was not so offended that she could no longer speak to him. And the only chance they had of speaking without being overheard was while walking in the park, with her maid trailing far behind.

SUSANNAH DRESSED IN the pink day dress her mother had selected, even though it was one she hated. She had tried in vain to avoid spending time alone with the earl, and now it was something she was going to have to face.

She felt so stupid for letting the earl's declaration—the declaration that he would not marry her, something she had been well aware of—upset her so much. She was not the type of young lady prone to hiding away in her room and crying, and yet that was what she had found herself doing over the last three days. Not because she had thought at any point that he would propose marriage…but because of how much it hurt to hear him declare that it certainly was not going to happen.

It was her own fault; she knew it. She had let her feelings for the earl grow far stronger than they had any right being. She had allowed herself to believe a lie—and then been hurt by reality.

Thankfully, her mother had seemed to believe her claim that she had a cold, and so she had been able to languish in her room for three days without having to see the earl or face the feelings in her treacherous heart.

But there was only so far she could take it. When her mother had insisted that the doctor must be called if she truly was so ill that she could not leave her room, Susannah had known she needed to return to her normal life.

She just hoped the time spent mourning her silly feelings would ensure that she did not make a fool of herself.

Lord Bourne was waiting by the front door when she descended the stairs. He looked as handsome as ever, and she felt a lump in her throat when she thought of the fact that one day he would surely find a beautiful, titled wife, who would get to live the life that Susannah had found herself daydreaming about.

In some ways, she cursed the day Lord Bourne had arrived at their house. For she had not known what she was missing before him.

But now… now she had tasted what her life could be. That one kiss had made the world shimmer, and without the possibility of it happening again, everything seemed dull.

She knew better than to think a man like the Earl of Bourne could ever be interested in her as more than a diversion to pass the time.

CHAPTER EIGHTEEN

"GOOD AFTERNOON," LORD Bourne said with a bow of his head.

"Good afternoon," Susannah replied, taking the proffered cloak from her maid, who was waiting, ready to chaperone them.

"We do not have to walk for long if you are feeling fatigued after your illness," Lord Bourne said as he put on his top hat and opened the front door. Sunlight streamed through, and Susannah followed him out, wishing he had offered her an out earlier in the day, when her mother had been present.

Except…except she didn't really. Because she didn't truly curse the day he had arrived, and she'd missed spending time with him—even though she knew it was bound to hurt her more in the end.

"Thank you." When he offered his arm, she took it. "I hope I can manage a little way. After all, I have been cooped up for days."

The day was fine, and the streets were busy, with everyone taking advantage of the nice weather to walk in St. James's Park, to see and be seen.

Louise kept her distance, and so it was almost as though they were alone.

But not alone like they had been the other night in the library. They would never be alone like that again.

"I hope you are truly feeling better," Lord Bourne said.

"I am, thank you." She knew she needed to remain polite and friendly, without allowing her heart to get any further engaged.

"I was concerned that…" he began, but then he trailed off. As intrigued as Susannah was, she did not press him. They were silent for a few moments, and then he tried again. "I wondered if, perhaps, you were not ill, exactly…"

Her heart began to race. She hadn't made her feelings obvious, had she? She did not want anyone—and most especially not the earl—to know she had spent three days upset in her room because a man she knew would never marry her had stated as much.

"I was ill," she insisted quickly.

"Ah. Forgive me then."

They walked a little further, the sunlight pleasant on her skin after days of being indoors. Susannah tried to think of a topic of conversation that might be neutral, that would not cause her heart to ache, that would not give away her stupid feelings.

"Did you manage to read much, while you were ill?" he asked. "Or perhaps make headway on your own novel?"

"I read, a little," she said, wishing she had never admitted her foolish notion of one day writing a novel. "My head was sore…" And in truth, reading about love and weddings and everything being right in the end hadn't been what her poor heart needed. She was sure she would get over it soon, and her books would bring her joy once more… Or she would choose some less romantic ones when she next ventured to the library.

Except how could she step into the library without thinking of him, and that kiss?

"I finished *Pride and Prejudice*," he said, and she couldn't help but look up at him, a smile taking over her lips.

"That was quick."

"It was very engaging," he said. "Another excellent recommendation."

"I'm glad you enjoyed it." Her heart felt lighter at the thought that he did care about her opinions. So he had no interest in marrying her—that wasn't a surprise. He still listened to what she had to say, and that was more than most.

THE CONVERSATION BETWEEN them was far more awkward than he had hoped, and he tried to steer it to easier ground. She smiled when he mentioned his reading, and that was something—but he still could not shake the fact that he had offended her. With the kiss.

The kiss that he couldn't seem to forget.

"I'm not sure whether I will stay in London for the entire Season," he said, more to see her reaction than anything else. If his presence was making her uncomfortable, he didn't want to inflict it on her for the weeks that were left of the Season.

He found he didn't particularly want to leave...but he thought remaining was possibly putting off his duties back at his estate in Kent.

And he wasn't sure his desire to stay was motivated by anything sensible.

"Oh," she said, her features falling for a second, before an impassive look took over her face once more. "You mentioned that before the Merriweather ball."

"I have a lot to attend to in the country..."

She nodded. "Of course."

Was she disappointed? Or simply remaining distant, as she had done since that kiss? Well, since she had felt ill at the ball, at least?

He couldn't tell...and he knew it didn't really matter. He enjoyed her company, and making her smile—but he had no plan to marry her. So he most certainly should not be entertaining staying in London because of her.

CHAPTER NINETEEN

"I THINK I will return to Kent earlier than I planned," Colin said, as he took tea with his aunt on a Tuesday afternoon.

"Oh?" She raised an eyebrow. "I thought you intended to sort everything with the lawyers and accountants, and make sure your social standing was intact, before you returned to the countryside."

He nodded. "I did. But I believe I have done all I can here—and the estate will still need to be dealt with, however long I put it off for."

"You put it off for years while you were off gallivanting across the globe," his aunt said with a sigh. "And if you go scurrying off to the countryside now, you'll only cause gossip. Everyone is expecting a marriage proposal from you before the Season is out."

Colin sipped his tea and did not comment. Things had become rather awkward between him and Miss Lyttleton since the kiss—which had not been mentioned since. He could only assume she was offended by his behavior, but it certainly made their arrangement less feasible, and less enjoyable. She didn't seem happy in his company, and he didn't wish to force her to endure it.

"You know how quickly gossip moves on, Aunt. They may wonder why I've left, but a few days later it will be someone else's name on their lips."

His aunt huffed. "I suppose. And is everything sorted with the men you needed to meet with in London? The estate is secure?"

"It will be," he said. "No thanks to my father…but I'm taking steps to ensure his choices will not affect the earls of the future."

"Once you have everything in order, your priority must be to find a suitable wife, Colin. To make sure there is an heir ready to take your place, when the time should come."

Colin sipped his tea to stop himself from sighing. "Yes, Aunt." He was well aware that he would need an heir—and he rather thought that was the reason his aunt had insisted he come back. Not entirely because of worries about the estate, but because she wished to ensure he chose a proper English wife, and got to work producing an heir.

No one wanted a bastard child from the continent causing issues—but Colin was confident that would not be the case. He had not lived like a monk, but he had been careful, not wanting to continue in his father's footsteps. When he did have children, they would be legitimate, and raised in a household where both mother and father were content. He had vowed that to himself a long time ago.

"Don't leave the Lyttleton girl heartbroken, will you. She may be plain, but she's sweet, and she doesn't deserve that."

Colin found himself gritting his teeth at her being called "plain", yet again. Why was everyone so quick to judge her? And why couldn't they see what lay beneath her supposedly plain looks?

"There is no risk of me breaking her heart, Aunt, do not worry."

COLIN HAD TAKEN to sitting in the library when he was spending time in the Lyttletons' home. It was a warm, cozy place—and not just because of the fire. He felt at ease there, whether alone or with the other inhabitants of the house.

With one particular inhabitant of the house…but he knew he shouldn't be thinking of her like that. Since she had not mentioned it, he was sure the right thing to do was to pretend it hadn't happened and move on from the strange feelings he'd been having.

Well, they weren't exactly strange—just unexpected. Miss Lyttleton was the bookish, spinster daughter of his host—nothing more. He had not anticipated feeling attracted to her, nor kissing her. He had never before taken such liberties with a woman who ought to be considered marriageable, even if society was rather blind to her qualities.

A knock on the door broke his reverie, and Simpkins, the butler, entered the room.

"Excuse me, Lord Bourne. There is a Mr. Lenton to see you. He says he is your lawyer."

Colin nodded. "Yes, he is. Would you show him in here, please?"

He did not like the fact that the lawyer was visiting him here. It suggested that something was wrong, for they had met at his office the previous time, and there had been no mention of a follow-up meeting.

"Indeed, my lord." With a sharp bow, Simpkins left the room and soon returned, accompanied by the small lawyer. Today he was wigless, his balding head sparsely covered by strands of graying hair. Without the wig he looked older, less confident— although perhaps that was also due to the change in setting.

"Can I get you some tea?" the butler asked.

"Yes, please," Colin said, glancing over at his lawyer, who was fiddling with his hands as though he were nervous. "And then, if you could see that we are not disturbed, I would much appreciate it."

When the butler left, and Lenton was still standing, Colin gestured toward an empty seat by the fireplace. "Please, sit. What can I do for you?"

Mr. Lenton perched on the edge of the chair, looking like he might flee at any moment. His nervousness was not helping the unease that grew in Colin's belly.

"I have been drawing up the paperwork as you requested, my lord," Mr. Lenton began. "And as part of it, I sent my assistant to one of the homes in question—the one in which the female recipient of the gift had died, and only her children were in residence."

"That was quick," Colin commented, not sure what else to say.

"This particular house is not far outside of London, and I thought it prudent to thoroughly know the lay of the land before writing up the paperwork."

"And? What did you discover?" Colin asked, feeling rather impatient to know what had brought the man here.

"Well," the lawyer said, twisting his hands together and avoiding the earl's gaze. "The eldest son living there, he is claiming... well, he—"

At that moment, a knock on the door announced the arrival of the tea, and the lawyer fell silent until the footman delivering it had closed the door again.

"Please, continue," Colin said through gritted teeth when the little man did not immediately resume where he had left off.

"Yes, indeed. The man in question is claiming to be the illegitimate son of your father, the late earl."

The words hung heavily in the air, though they were not the shock that the lawyer seemed to think they would be. After all, Colin was well aware that his father had had many, many affairs. It would surely be foolish to think none of them had resulted in a pregnancy.

"Did my father acknowledge him?"

The lawyer shook his head. "Not as far as I can tell. And of course, there is no way to know for sure..."

"No, there is not. We only have his word for it, with the other parties long gone." Colin sighed. This was yet another issue stemming from his father's very messy life. Children were born not knowing who their parents truly were, with nothing provided for them, as would have been if they were legitimate.

"Does it give him any more rights to the home than if he were not making such a claim?"

"No. Even if he could prove he was an illegitimate son, he would have no rights. Of course, he might decide to use such information, to spread it for his own gain, or to try to extort money from you…"

"My father's sins are no secret. They are nothing to do with me, and if this man wishes to spread this information, I will not pay a penny to stop him."

The lawyer nodded. "Yes, of course. I have worked on cases similar to this, where an amount of money has been settled upon the party claiming parentage, in order to leave such things in the past."

"And what then is there to stop a hundred other such men or women from claiming the exact same thing? And taking as much money from the estate as possible? We both know—in fact, much of society knows—that my father had such relationships with many, many women. There is a large age range of children who could potentially be his, but whom he never claimed, and whom he never sought to provide for. I'm not sure that that should be my responsibility."

"Understood, my lord."

"I do not wish to be cruel. I am happy for him to continue living there—but if his descendants wish to, they will need to pay an appropriate rent. I think that is fair."

"Exceedingly so, my lord," the lawyer said. "I will get this put in writing, and see that it is signed. I am sorry to have to burden you with such knowledge—"

"It is my father who has burdened me, and all those he took to his bed," Colin said bitterly, the tear-stained face of his mother floating in his mind. He had always wanted a brother, and she had always looked longingly at large families. Had she known that the old earl potentially had other children? Did it add to the heartache?

And did this man, whoever he was, truly believe his father was the old earl? Or was he trying his luck?

Not for the first time, Colin cursed his father, and the mess he had left behind.

CHAPTER TWENTY

W HEN MR. LYTTLETON asked him into the study for a drink after supper, Colin readily agreed. His host asked very little of him, and he was happy to do him this courtesy, even if he wasn't sure they had much to discuss.

"Port or whiskey?" Mr. Lyttleton asked as the door swung closed.

"Whiskey, please." Colin took a seat in the large red wing-back chair that sat opposite Mr. Lyttleton's desk. It was not a room he had frequented often since his arrival, preferring the library, and as he glanced around, he noticed how neat it was and how much paperwork Mr. Lyttleton had piled upon his desk. He was clearly a very busy man, with numerous involvements in his businesses, despite having already made so much money.

"Are you enjoying the Season, Lord Bourne?" Mr. Lyttleton asked, sliding a glass of whiskey across the desk to him and taking his own seat.

"Please, just call me Bourne," Colin said, feeling a little un-comfortable standing on ceremony when he was living in this man's home. "And yes, it has been pleasantly diverting—more so than I had expected, I must admit."

"I'm glad to hear it. Although I have heard talk that you may leave before the Season is over?"

Colin swallowed his sip of whiskey more quickly than was sensible and had to cough before he answered. "I—" He couldn't tell Mr. Lyttleton that things weren't so enjoyable since he had kissed the man's daughter and now things were awkward between them. He didn't even want to admit how big a part of his reasoning that was.

"My estate has been long-neglected. I thought not to return to it until after the Season, but I do wonder now whether I am putting it off without good reason. I may have been earl for some time, but I have not been in the country nor taken responsibility for my estates. Now seems the time to do so."

For a moment, Mr. Lyttleton simply nodded without saying anything. "I understand," he eventually added. "And I commend your sense of duty—I do. But I feel we must talk, before you leave, about my daughter."

Colin froze in the chair, wondering if Mr. Lyttleton knew, wondering if he was about to call him out. And he knew he would deserve such treatment too—he had not behaved in a gentlemanly way toward Miss Lyttleton.

Had she told him? He couldn't quite imagine her doing so, especially so many days after the fact. But the truth was that Mr. Lyttleton wanted to talk about her, and Colin had no escape.

"Indeed," Colin finally managed to say, as his mind reached for excuses and reasons but came up short.

"You have singled her out this Season. And do not think we are not grateful; she has been on the marriage market for some time, and the interest of a man such as yourself—"

Colin bit the inside of his lip to stop himself from saying something. He knew it wasn't his place to say so, but he really did not like the way they spoke of Susannah. Of course, he knew she had been looking for a husband for some time, but she didn't need her parents disseminating that information, surely.

"But what I need to know is," Mr. Lyttleton said, tapping his fingers on the side of his glass of whiskey as though the conversation was quite awkward for him, "what your intentions are. Your names have been linked, as I'm sure you are aware. The dances, the promenades… If you were to disappear to the country now, it would look as though my daughter had done something wrong." Mr. Lyttleton narrowed his eyes. "And I presume she has not."

Colin quickly shook his head. "No, no—she has done nothing wrong." It was he who had done something wrong—but it seemed Mr. Lyttleton was not aware of it. He simply wished to know what Colin planned regarding his daughter, which was a question Colin ought to have been expecting.

When the time came, they had agreed that Miss Lyttleton would be the one to break it off...but of course, Colin could not tell her father that and out the whole courtship as a lie.

"Your daughter is a very charming young lady," Colin said, speaking without telling a single lie. "I am very much enjoying the time I spend with her...but I feel I must tell you that I'm not ready to wed just yet."

There, Colin thought to himself. *That ought to surely placate him a little. And if he wants to warn me off her, then I can keep my distance. If I'm returning home anyway, I shan't see her anymore.*

He was surprised at the wave of sadness that washed over him at the thought of not seeing her again. He was aware that he found her, perhaps rather surprisingly, attractive. He had initiated that kiss, he was sure of it—and if the lightning had not interrupted them, he was rather concerned he would have taken things further.

"I understand. You are a young man, and you have been traveling the world. I can see why you might not wish to tie yourself down just yet. But I must ask you to think of my daughter's reputation. I am, of course, aware that she is a plain girl and that she is unlikely to be chosen for her looks—"

At this, Colin pulled one hand into a fist in his lap; the other tightened around his whiskey glass. They spoke of her as if she were some kind of old hag. When really, Colin had seen a beauty in her that only grew with each day.

"I think she is perfectly capable of securing a husband with her looks," he interrupted as politely as he could manage.

Mr. Lyttleton looked at him skeptically and pursed his lips

before continuing. "Well. She should certainly be able to attract a husband with the size of her dowry. But if her reputation were impacted by you suddenly leaving, and people thinking it was her fault…"

"I can assure you that I will not leave Miss Lyttleton's reputation with a stain upon it," Colin promised. After all, aside from the kiss, he planned to leave her a more attractive prospect to future husbands, not less. And no one ever needed to know about the kiss.

Mr. Lyttleton smiled. "Excellent. I am pleased to hear it. And may I just say, whether you stay for the rest of the Season or only briefly, what a pleasure it has been for us to host you."

"And I appreciate your hospitality," Colin said, feeling like he might say something rude if he stayed much longer. The way they spoke of Susannah, as if she were incapable of finding a husband, as if she were nothing but a problem to be solved…it made him angry. He stood, placing his empty glass on the desk more forcefully than he had intended.

"If you'll excuse me, I have some correspondence I must see to before I retire." Colin did not wait for Mr. Lyttleton to agree. Instead, he stalked from the room and made his way straight to his chamber, where he would not be disturbed.

Why was he so angry? Miss Lyttleton was not his wife, and she was their daughter. Even if he did not like it, there was no reason for them to worry about how they discussed her because of his views.

He would make sure that in not marrying her, he made it very clear it was not her fault—and he firmly believed that his interest, and her unavailability, would only make her more appealing to prospective husbands.

And yet…

He banged his fist on the dressing table, just to have something to do to ease his anger. Dammit, but the thought of her wedded to someone else made him angry too. He was attracted to her, he felt something for her, he could not deny it.

But what he had said to Mr. Lyttleton was not entirely a lie. He was not ready to marry. The estate needed far too much organization for him to focus on a wife. And he would not be his father, breaking the heart of the woman he had legally wed with his negligence and inattention.

And at the back of his mind, he knew his aunt had had a point when she had said that Miss Lyttleton was not the sort of woman he should be marrying. Not because of her looks or society's perception of them. Not because she came from a more modern family. No, because he needed someone who could be a countess, who could restore the reputation of the Bourne title, and Colin wasn't sure Susannah had the confidence to do so.

CHAPTER TWENTY-ONE

S USANNAH TURNED THE final page of the novel she had been devouring that week, and let out a sigh of delight. She loved when everything was satisfyingly tied up at the end of the novel, a conclusion which real life seemed to so often be lacking.

The fire in the grate had almost died out, and the house was quiet. Her mother and father had gone to bed over an hour earlier, and she had promised she wasn't far behind—but it was too tempting to stay in the comfortable chair she had been occupying in the parlor and finish her book, even though her eyelids were beginning to droop.

The novel—*The Mysteries of Udolhpo*—had given her more ideas for stories that she wished to pen herself. Feeling inspired, she hurried over to the bureau in the corner, took out a sheet of parchment from a stack which her mother kept there for corresponding, and a quill and ink, and began to scribble furiously. The market day scene she wrote was something she had witnessed many times before, except she had added a twist: an orphaned girl was about to be kidnapped, and her life set on a very different path.

She wondered if her scribblings—which were locked away in the drawer of her bureau, for she would have been mortified if anyone had ever discovered them and read them—would be more interesting if she had lived a more exciting life. If she had traveled, and seen some of the world, as Lord Bourne had done, then perhaps the settings for her stories would not simply be London, or the English countryside.

But she hadn't ever even been to Scotland, and she doubted she would travel any further than her aunt's home in Peterborough, which they occasionally visited, unless she somehow ended up marrying a man from further afield.

Or marrying at all.

The candle at the bureau flickered and guttered, and she stopped writing as the room grew dark. The light from the dying fire was not enough to see by, and she knew she ought to go to bed, and not light another one, as much as her imagination was fired up. They were to call on her mother's friends in the morning, and though it would not be a particularly early start, her mother would be able to tell if she had stayed up too late reading or writing. She always could, somehow. And then Susannah wouldn't hear the end of it.

She blew on the parchment, hoping to dry the ink quicker so it would not run, and then folded it before padding from the room. The candles in the sconces were still burning, and so she knew not all the staff had gone to bed, but the hallway was deserted.

The library door had been left ajar, and she could see a fire had been lit in there, too, and was presumably dying out now like her own in the parlor. She passed the door, thinking how tired she suddenly felt, when she heard humming, and froze.

Who was still up?

And why was she so drawn to the sound? She knew the answers to both questions of course: Lord Bourne. He was awake as he had been before, and it was he whose humming she heard.

Without thinking about whether it was a good idea, she pushed the door open and found the Earl of Bourne sitting before the fireplace, humming to himself with his eyes closed.

He clearly hadn't heard her enter and for a moment she just watched him. She had been struck by how handsome he was on the very first day he had entered the parlor, but relaxed like this, he was almost beautiful. His head was tilted back, leaving the column of his neck exposed to her gaze, lit by the firelight. His lips were slightly parted, reminding her of their kiss and his taste. An unexpected urge to run her own lips over the hard angle of his jaw and chin, over the masculine ridge of his Adam's apple and down to the soft hollow of his throat struck her, though she didn't know why that was so appealing, nor why the thought of it made her breath catch or her knees weak.

She knew she shouldn't be there. That they should not be alone together. That standing and staring at him as the shadows from the fire danced across his face was very inappropriate behavior indeed.

But she couldn't help herself.

Nor could she stop the unexpected sneeze which came upon her without warning. She tried to quell it, but doing so only made it louder, and when she opened her eyes, his own were open too, and staring at her in shock.

"I'm sorry," she squeaked, gripping the folded piece of parchment in her hand tightly. "I didn't mean—"

"I thought everyone was asleep," he said, sitting upright but not standing.

"I was just finishing my book. I…heard you humming."

He screwed up his face a little. "Was I?"

She nodded. "I didn't recognize the tune…"

His eyes glazed over, as if trying to remember. "I can't even continue the tune. I didn't realize I was doing it."

Feeling a little silly, she nevertheless found herself still standing in the doorway, attempting to hum the same tune which had drawn her into the room.

His face softened, and his eyes filled with emotion.

"I haven't heard that in a long time. I didn't realize I still remembered it…"

She stepped into the room and then pushed the library door closed, telling herself it was as inappropriate as staring at him, but that it needed to be done to keep the heat from the fire in the room—even though it hadn't needed to be done initially, for she'd been standing in an open doorway after all. She pushed such logical thoughts aside. She was tired of thinking, of always doing what was expected. Tonight was a night for doing the unexpected. So she asked, "Where is it from?" before walking a little closer, so she could speak without raising her voice.

"My mother used to sing it to me, when I was a child," he said, the ghost of a smile passing across his face. "I cannot remember the lyrics, but the tune is unmistakable."

She smiled and took a step closer. She knew she ought to go to bed, to remove herself from being alone in his presence. *Just look at what had happened the last time.*

But no one knew about it. And they had pretended like nothing had happened.

So she needed to make sure nothing happened again.

Even if she secretly rather wanted it to.

They had not spoken without an awkward air surrounding them since she had heard him loudly proclaim he would never marry her, and she found she missed the easy conversations. She missed him…which she didn't think made much sense, since she had only known him a few short weeks.

But in spite of all of that, she *did* miss him. And the urge to sit and converse with him, just for a short while, without anyone around to judge them or what they said, or how they behaved was too great to ignore.

CHAPTER TWENTY-TWO

COLIN RAN A hand through his hair, feeling a little groggy. He had closed his eyes for a moment, even though he did not feel ready for bed, and when he had opened them, she had had been standing there. And then she had hummed that tune, and so many memories had come flooding back. Memories of his Mama, and the love she showed him, and how she cared for him.

Memories of how his father never made her happy, in spite of all her efforts to make sure the household ran smoothly and that he was never burdened.

Belatedly, he realized that he had not stood up when Miss Lyttleton had entered the room, and that they were alone again, in the very same place where that kiss had occurred.

The kiss that shouldn't have happened.

The kiss that had been on his mind far more often than he would ever admit.

"It's very late," he said, feeling like he needed to remind himself what was expected of him. He was an earl, and she was a gentleman's daughter, and it was not a good idea for him to forget it.

She was still dressed in the simple pink dress she had worn for dinner, her glossy brown hair plaited down her back. Her honey-amber eyes glinted in the firelight, and he was overwhelmed with the desire to kiss her again, and he knew his heart—and somewhere rather south of his heart—was in danger of overruling his head.

This was a very bad idea, but he couldn't bring himself to care about that.

"I know," she said, taking another step towards him. "But I find I am not tired."

He swallowed, and his gaze wandered down her pale neck, to the neckline of her dress, which just hinted at the creamy breasts beneath. When she had been in here in her nightdress, much more of her had been on display, and yet he found himself just as attracted to her now, in her plain dress—a dress he was sure was one of her older ones, for it did not have the lower neckline of her newer acquisitions.

His mind was wandering further into dangerous territory still, and yet he could not stop it.

"If you want to sit, for a while," he said, gesturing to the empty chair in front of him. "And read, or talk...the fire is still warm."

She didn't hesitate to take the seat before him. Her knees were mere inches away from his, and she had no book to read, although she did have a piece of parchment clutched in her fingertips.

"A letter from a paramour?" he asked with a glance towards it.

She laughed. "That seems rather unlikely."

He frowned. "You do yourself a disservice. There is no reason, Miss Lyttleton, why you should not attract a good husband."

"I have not so far," she said softly, but without bitterness. Indeed, she sounded almost bored by the topic. Perhaps she was, for her parents, at least, seemed to harp on the topic almost ceaselessly. "And I regularly hear reasons why I won't, or will never. From many speakers."

Colin thought back to the cruel gossips in the ballroom.

"People are fools."

She shrugged, a gesture which was unladylike and casual— something of which he was sure her mother would disapprove. But it showed him she felt comfortable in his presence, something that warmed his heart. "Father believes someone will take me for my dowry."

"Yes, it might be an incentive," Colin agreed. "But I am confident, Miss Lyttleton—"

"Susannah," she interrupted, biting her lip immediately after as if the word had slipped out without her intent.

"Susannah," he repeated, the word feeling forbidden on his lips, and yet, so right. "I am confident, Susannah, that when the right man takes the time to speak with you, to get to know you, there will be no need of a large dowry to sway him. You…" He bit his lip. Good Lord, he'd nearly told her that while she was perhaps not conventionally pretty, he found her attractive, and even admitted that she cast some spell on him that he did not understand and could not escape.

It was as if he had spoken the words aloud, for her cheeks flushed red, and she glanced to the floor. Her fingers appeared to clasp tighter around the piece of parchment.

"So if it is not a letter from a love-sick gentleman, what is it that you hold on to so tightly?" he asked, reaching out to touch the parchment, to illustrate his point, to perhaps brush his fingers against hers…

She pulled back quickly, her head snapping up and her eyes meeting his and her cheeks turning even redder, if such a thing were possible. "Nothing."

Now his curiosity was certainly piqued. "Nothing?"

"It's…" She looked into the fire, and then back at him. "Nothing I wish to share."

He nodded, and then leant back in his chair. "Your father asked me about my intentions toward you," he said, changing the subject entirely.

Her eyes widened, and he wondered if she was thinking the same as he had when Mr. Lyttleton had cornered him—that he knew about the kiss.

"He has heard of my plans to leave before the Season is over, and was concerned I might damage your reputation, since it has become clear we have an…attachment."

The attachment was false, and so there was no reason for Colin to feel as awkward as he did. mentioning it.

"Ah," she said, her tongue darting out to wet her lips. Colin's body responded to her innocent action, and he shifted in the chair. "Well. I'm glad he is concerned…I suppose we do need a plausible story for the reason for our courtship has come to an end. When it does."

"I am happy to be entirely the party at fault," he said. "Perhaps…my constant discussion of my travels bored you to tears. Or you found me too vain to take seriously. Or my behavior was uncouth, due to me living abroad for so many years…"

She laughed softly and leaned forward. "I don't know if those lies will convince anyone who has met you this Season, Lord Bourne."

"Colin." She had, after all, told him to use her Christian name, and so it only seemed right to offer the same courtesy.

Politeness—that was all there was to it.

She blushed prettily, and smiled up at him. "Colin…your stories are always interesting, and while you are handsome, you are never vain. And your manners are perfect, as I'm sure you are aware."

He couldn't resist. As foolish as it was, as wrong as it was, he leaned forward and pressed his lips to hers…and she immediately kissed him back.

Their bodies met in the space between the two armchairs, and as he laid her down on the rug before the fireplace, all he was thinking was that she was intoxicating, and he needed more of her.

CHAPTER TWENTY-THREE

SUSANNAH COULD NEVER, in her wildest dreams, have imagined that this would happen when she'd entered the library door. His kiss was hungry, scorching, desperate, and she matched his passion, swept up in the moment.

He covered her body with his, and she felt breathless—not just from his weight atop her, but from everything moving so fast, from his lips upon hers, from not knowing what was to come.

His lips moved to her neck, her clavicle, trailing a fiery line of kisses until he reached the swell of her breasts, which were barely visible in this dress. She rather wished she was just in her nightgown, as she had been the last time she had stumbled across him in the library—and then was shocked at such a wanton thought.

She gasped at the sensation of his lips on the delicate, bare skin of her décolletage, and writhed beneath him as one hand moved to cup her left breast through the dress.

"Susannah," he murmured, his breath hot against her skin. She felt like she might explode at any moment, the heat within her more powerful than any coming from the fire they were laying before.

She had some idea of what happened between a husband and wife, from reading books that were surely not meant for her eyes, but she'd had no idea it could feel like this. Or that she could lose all sense of time and place and propriety as his fingers trailed up her legs, pushed her skirts out of the way, and gently caressed that place between her thighs that was crying out for him.

"Colin," she groaned, unable to stop herself, pleasure building throughout her body.

And then he froze. His lips remained against her throat, his hand beneath her skirts, but he did not move, until he slowly pulled away.

"I—" he began, and Susannah's racing heart fell at the tortured look in his eyes. She pulled down her skirt, feeling suddenly very exposed, and pushed herself up on her elbows.

"Please, forgive me," he said, standing and walking towards the window. "I cannot do this."

Humiliation and horror swept over Susannah, making her stomach tighten and her skin flame. She scrambled to her feet and tried to make herself look presentable, even though she did not have a looking glass to check the results. She had almost given herself to him…and yet, he could not go through with it.

Had he really found her so unattractive that he could not proceed?

She felt her eyes filling with tears and she turned toward the door, refusing to let him see how upset he had made her—although he wasn't looking at her, anyway. He was staring out of the window, presumably horrified by what he had nearly done. And especially, that he'd nearly done it with *her*.

So why was she standing there, waiting for him to acknowledge her?

He didn't want her. That was clear enough. Something about her was so repulsive that he could not lie with her, and it broke her heart to think that he viewed her so.

She knew she wasn't pretty, but she'd thought he liked her, at least a little.

Well, apparently not enough.

She turned on her heel, deciding waiting was foolish, and wanting to escape to her room before the tears began to fall.

And then he called her name. Softly.

"Susannah..."

She could not help but turn around, even though it hurt to even look at him. Her embarrassment crushed her, pressing on her shoulders, and wrapping around her middle. It choked her throat, made tears prick at her eyes. She was embarrassed about what she had almost done, embarrassed that he had called it off, embarrassed that she just wanted to cry.

"I'm sorry," he said, and although the words sounded sincere, they couldn't change what had happened.

She had no words to answer. They were stuck in her throat. So she turned back to the door, and hurried away, hoping desperately that she did not meet anyone on her way to bed.

COLIN HATED HIMSELF. He could see the hurt and confusion in her eyes, and yet there was nothing he could say but "sorry".

And she ran from the room anyway.

He didn't blame her. It was probably the most sensible thing she'd done all evening. After all, he had not behaved like a gentleman at all. What he'd begun with her was totally wrong— and it had only been the sound of his name, falling from her lips, that had made him pause, to think about what he was doing.

And he couldn't continue.

Not just because she was an innocent, or that she was a proper young lady—although both were certainly reasons why he should not have deflowered her on the library floor—but because he had vowed not to be like his father.

He would not have a bevy of mistresses, he would not leave a trail of illegitimate children in his wake. He would marry, and he would be faithful.

He could not ruin Miss Lyttleton, Susannah, in that way. He would not behave like that, even if he had forgotten himself briefly. He had treated her poorly, and he only hoped she would forgive him. He would have to try to apologize to her properly the following day, for it was certainly not appropriate for him to go to her bedchamber, especially now—and he wasn't totally sure he could resist the temptation if he did.

Downing the last of his brandy, he blew out the candles and made his way to bed. He did not want to spend hours sitting in the library, regretting what he had done…or wishing he had not had an attack of conscience.

His attraction to Miss Lyttleton was driving him to distraction, and that was certainly not something he had expected when he had first arrived.

CHAPTER TWENTY-FOUR

SUSANNAH REGARDED HER reflection in the looking glass. There was nothing she could do about her red eyes. If her mother and father asked, she would have to say that she had another cold, or perhaps hay fever. But Colin—Lord Bourne—would surely know it was because she had been crying.

There was nothing to be done. She had to see him, had to speak to him, had to bring whatever this mess was to a close. He had made her believe, just for a moment, that she was not undesirable. That she was not as plain, boring, and unappealing as she had spent her life believing and being told.

And then, in a cruel second, he had doubled all her doubts about herself.

She knew she should be furious with him for compromising her, for almost taking her innocence. She knew she should be angry at herself for breaking all the rules she had been raised to follow.

But all she felt was heartbreak. Heartbreak at the reality that she had been willing to do anything for him, to compromise her morals, to throw away her virtue—and even then, he could not bring himself to go through with it.

How on earth was she ever to have a husband if, even in such a situation, she could not entice a man to bed?

Tears began to fill her eyes again, and she squeezed them tightly shut, forbidding them to fall.

It was done. Her heart was broken. She had realized just how deeply she had fallen for him just as he stuck the knife in. And perhaps it was even love. Whatever it was, it was certainly powerful, overwhelming, and totally and utterly pointless.

She descended the stairs, giving herself a stern talking-to, and then sought him out in the library, where he so often was. When she opened the door, she could not help but glance at the rug on the floor by the fireplace, where she had so nearly…

No. It hurt too much to think of it. She turned away and found him sitting on the other side of the room, his legs crossed, his cravat slightly loosened. His eyes widened, and he stood, tossing the book he had been reading onto the chaise longue behind him.

"Susannah," he said, taking two steps toward her. "I must apologize. I need to explain. Last night was unforgivable—"

Susannah held up her hand to silence him. She was not surprised that he felt bad for almost seducing her. Especially if he had thought through the consequences and was currently contemplating the fact that, had they been caught, he would have almost certainly been forced to marry her.

But she did not want to hear apologies or excuses. She did not regret the near events, except for the fact that they had broken her heart. She did not expect him to marry her, and she was not here to demand any discussion on the topic. She simply needed this to be over, for both of their sakes, before she ended up ruined. For if she were brokenhearted and unmarriageable, that would surely be an even worse situation.

"Our arrangement must come to an end, Lord Bourne," she said, even though in her head she thought he would always be Colin. "Our pretense served its purpose, and you have not been bothered by other young ladies of the ton. But, with recent events, I think you must agree that the ruse must be terminated."

He opened and shut his mouth several times without saying anything, and she congratulated herself on getting through her prepared speech without faltering and without crying.

"I must apologize—"

"There is nothing to apologize for. We were both at fault, and I understand that you were simply... caught up in the moment. But the point of this arrangement was to keep the marriage-minded ladies away from you and give me time to read in peace without my parents worrying about my prospects. And I believe we have been successful in both those aims. But now... I must find a husband. And your presence here is only risking my reputation."

She held her head high and squeezed her nails into the palm of her hand to stop herself from crying. She did not really believe that finding a husband was a likely outcome, but it seemed a better reason to give him for the need for him to depart than that he had broken her heart. That his disgust in her physical appearance was more painful than she could possibly have imagined.

She never wished to admit that to him, or to anyone.

"But—"

"You spoke of leaving to return to your estates earlier than planned. I think, given the circumstances, that is for the best. I wish you well, Lord Bourne."

And with a nod of her head, she strode from the room, not able to look at him for a moment longer. She knew her resolve was in danger of weakening, that at any moment she might listen to what he had to say, that she might think it made sense, that she might fall into his arms and then be humiliated all over again. And she couldn't handle that. She might be plain, but she had her pride—or at least she wanted to have it. And so she needed to be away from him.

Even if that hurt, too.

COLIN HALF FELL, half-stumbled back into his armchair. He didn't know what he had expected from her. Perhaps that she would shout or be angry with him for his ungentlemanly behavior. Perhaps that she would cry and insist they wed since he had come so close to taking her virtue.

In fact, the outcome he had thought most likely was that she would ignore the situation entirely and pretend it didn't happen—just like with the kiss.

But he had not expected this cold, determined woman to tell him it was time for him to leave.

He sat alone in the library for quite some time, contemplating his options. He had obviously deeply offended her, and his ungentlemanly behavior had ruined any sort of friendship there could have been between them.

Had she demanded they wed, he thought there was a chance he would have agreed. Not because he was ready for marriage or because he thought he was in a position to be a good husband, but because he had been raised to do the right thing. And in the library the previous night, he had come very close to doing the wrong thing.

He would not be like his father. He would not lay with an innocent woman before marriage. He would not sire a string of illegitimate children, who would then spend their lives not knowing their place in the world, feeling abandoned, feeling resentful toward him.

And he did not want to break a woman's heart. Especially once he was married.

But she had not demanded marriage. In fact, although her eyes had been red and looked as though she had been crying, she did not look particularly upset—more angry if anything. She did not look like she had any wish to wed him, no matter the circumstances.

She wanted to find a proper husband. And she deserved that. He owed her that, after everything.

The clock struck eleven, and he forced himself from his chair. He was almost certain he had missed the rest of the family breaking their fast, which had been intentional. He could not sit opposite Susannah and act entirely normally. But hunger was beginning to affect him, so he left his sanctuary to seek out some food.

She had told him it was time to leave, and he felt his only option was to take her at her word.

After all, the charade clearly could not continue now, and he wasn't sure they could even be cordial to one another. And if his presence really was damaging her chances of finding a husband, he knew it was only right to remove himself.

By the time he entered the dining room, his mind was made up. He would leave by the end of the week and try to forget about Susannah Lyttleton and the way she had surprisingly caught his attention to the point where all he thought of was her.

He rang the bell, and the footman appeared speedily.

"Good morning, my lord."

"Good morning. Could you please have some bread and cheese sent up? I missed breakfast."

The footman bowed his head. "Of course, my lord."

"And please ask my valet to come and find me as soon as he can."

The valet ended up arriving before the bread and cheese, and Colin set out his plan. "I'll need you to pack my things so that we can depart on Friday. I shall hire a coach or borrow one—there's no reason to purchase one, since there are at least two at the estate, according to the ledgers."

If his valet was surprised by the sudden change in travel plans, he did not make it apparent. "Yes, my lord."

"We will have to stay at inns along the way, so perhaps you can send word. And arrange for some provisions from Cook so we do not have to stop more than is necessary."

Colin thought he would be relieved to have a plan in place, but once his valet had departed to do his bidding and his bread and cheese had arrived, he only felt sad.

He had let himself down the previous night, behaved in a

manner that was not suitable for an earl, and had let Susannah down too. And now he was to return to an old house that held some rather painful memories—a house he had not lived in for at least fifteen years. He had no idea what state it was even in. He needed to check whether any of the staff had been retained or whether he would have to hire an entirely new staff once he arrived.

He had come to London first and stayed with the Lyttletons to ease himself back into society. And yet now he felt as though he was heading into the countryside completely alone, to face his past and determine his future.

He had spent a lot of time alone throughout the years. But over the Season, he had grown rather used to living within a family. Granted, they weren't his family, but they had been welcoming and kind and present.

And it was harder than he imagined to just walk away.

CHAPTER TWENTY-FIVE

SUSANNAH WATCHED COLIN leave from her bedroom window that Friday morning. They had said their goodbyes at dinner the previous night, with him giving his heartfelt thanks for allowing him to stay.

Her goodbye had been just the same as the one for her mother and father. Of course, it had to be. He could hardly kiss her in front of them. And she shouldn't want that either. She had told him to leave, and he was clearly not attracted to her—not in the way a man ought to be toward a woman.

This morning, as she watched his borrowed carriage riding away, she did not hold back her tears. This was the right decision, she was sure—but that didn't mean it didn't hurt. There was a good chance she would never see him again, and it broke her heart to think that.

Still, she needed to make herself presentable before going downstairs. She did not want her parents questioning why she was so upset. Of course, they had believed there was some connection between her and Colin, but they also very easily believed it when nothing came of it.

So, it would look strange if she appeared distraught at his departure.

She just needed to move on.

At luncheon, however, all her parents spoke of was Colin. There was no escaping him, even now he had left.

"Such a nice young man," her mother said.

"Yes, I'm sure he will do well in life. He's got a talent for making people like him, no matter their background. But he seems genuine too, don't you think?" her father asked.

"Oh, most definitely."

Susannah managed to stay out of the conversation until her parents decided she ought to join in.

"I am sorry things did not progress between the two of you," Mama said, with a smile that Susannah presumed was meant to be comforting. "It would have been a fine, if ambitious, match."

"Yes, Mother," Susannah said, for what else was there to say?

"But you mustn't be downcast. There is still some of the Season left, and you may find that interest from the earl has increased your desirability, along with your large dowry. There is still hope, Susannah—don't despair."

Susannah nodded but did not trust herself to speak. Clearly, she was not doing as good a job at hiding her emotions as she had thought. But her mother thought she was sad at the prospect of never marrying—not for the very specific reason that she would never see Colin again.

That she wouldn't get to marry him—although surely that had never been on the cards anyway.

She had just allowed herself to think it might be a possibility, especially after he kissed her. Especially after that night in the library, on the rug in front of the fireplace, when they had so nearly…

"But I've said before, you cannot spend your time holed up in here reading. When the earl was showing interest in you, you could take a more relaxed view of the Season. But with him gone, we must press on."

It was exactly as it had been before Colin had arrived, or perhaps even worse. Her mother's vigor in pushing her onto the social scene and finding her a husband seemed renewed by the earl's passing interest.

And so she would have even less time to read and even more

opportunity to see that look in a gentleman's eyes when he felt he had to dance with her but had no real wish to.

It has come to this author's attention that Lord B has quit the Season early and returned to his country seat. Has he grown tired of the newfound wealth of his hosts? Rumors of a betrothal between him and Miss L now seem unfounded. In fact, the on dits in some ballrooms is that she broke off the attachment because he did not understand society manners well enough! Hopefully, Miss L will quickly find a match to rival him, although perhaps it is because of such high expectations that she remains unwed still.

Susannah rarely read the gossip columns, but in the days after Colin left, she found herself with much time in which she needed to be distracted, and a reason to take an interest in what the anonymous pens of the ton had to say.

She wasn't wholly surprised to see the reference to her and Colin's courtship, nor the fact that his lack of society knowledge was given as the reason for their connection ending. It had been one of his suggestions, after all. And she supposed he had put the word about before he had left.

In some ways, he seemed such a decent man. And yet he seemed to be totally repulsed by her…

She did not like to be the topic of gossip. While spending time with Colin had made the increased attention she received acceptable, she was more than happy to disappear into the background once more. She would try to attract a husband, because it was what her parents wanted, but she had no wish to have all eyes of the ton upon her.

Especially without Colin by her side.

What was he doing now, she found herself wondering, as she and Mama sat in silence completing their needlework. Was he happy to be at his estate? Was he relieved he had escaped the Season without being marched down the aisle?

Did he think of her at all?

Mama looked over at the fabric clutched in her hands and tutted. "That last row is very messy, Susannah. You will have to unpick it and do it again."

Without arguing, Susannah followed her mother's instructions. She didn't care about the needlework. She wished it engrossed her enough to take her mind off Colin, and the haunted look in his eye when he had told her he could not continue...but nothing seemed to be able to distract her from that.

Not even her beloved books.

"You need to get your head out of the clouds, Susannah. Men are looking for wives who have mastered the feminine arts—not ones who can read a book in a day. That will not interest them at all."

But it had interested Colin, Susannah wanted to say. He had always seemed to care about what she had to say—and he certainly hadn't acted like he cared a fig whether she could complete a neat row of cross stitch.

But perhaps it had all been an act. Perhaps he had feigned interest in her, and in the books of Miss Austen. It had all been a game of pretend, and she was the one who had ended up hurt.

And Colin...Lord Bourne... She sighed to herself as she unpicked the last of the stitches. He had probably forgotten all about her the moment the carriage pulled away from the city.

CHAPTER TWENTY-SIX

WHEN THE CARRIAGE pulled up outside his estate, Colin did not feel a sense of coming home. This place had been his childhood home, and he did have some good memories here. But they were from so long ago that they had been overtaken by others—ones he would rather forget.

His mother had died in this house. He and his father had argued endlessly in this house. He had walked away from this house at the age of eighteen, not knowing that when he returned, he would be the earl.

From the outside, it looked in fairly decent shape, and as the carriage came to a standstill, the small remaining crew of staff assembled in the courtyard, lined up to greet him.

The footman opened the door, and Colin emerged into the gray light of the day. He looked up at the building and suppressed a shiver. He did not want this to be his home. As much as his mother had tried to make his childhood a happy one, this was not a home that had been filled with love, happiness, or laughter. His mother had certainly loved him, but she had been so unhappy, and she had struggled not to let it show.

When he started a family, he wanted to do it right. He wanted a home full of joy, a wife who was at least content, and children who knew what love felt like.

An elderly man stepped forward out of the line, and Colin was surprised that he recognized him. The man gave a shaky bow and said, "Welcome back, my lord."

"Anderson! Goodness me. I have to admit, I did not expect to see you still at the helm."

Anderson gave a smile that lit up his face. "I have been butler here for forty years now, my lord. And I hope to remain so until I am incapable of fulfilling my duties."

"I am very glad to see the place in such good hands, especially since I have been away for so long."

"Thank you, my lord. We are running on rather a small staff, as you can see. But we keep things to the highest standard we possibly can."

"I have no doubt."

The rest of the assembled staff bowed or curtsied, and then the two footmen hurried to collect his cases from the carriage.

"The carriage will need to be returned to London, Anderson. I borrowed it from my hosts, the Lyttletons. If we have no one to spare to take it back, could you see to hiring someone from the village?"

"Of course, my lord. I will see to it straightaway. The master chamber is ready for you, and Cook has prepared luncheon for whenever you are hungry."

How odd it felt to be giving the orders in this place where he had always been expected to do as he was told. To know that each of those lofty rooms belonged to him.

Had his father and mother expected to fill those chambers with a brood of children, rather than the sole son they ended up with?

Well, his mother had a sole son. The number of children the old earl had was best left shrouded in mystery.

He half-expected ghosts to jump out at him as he entered the old building and ascended the staircase. Perhaps his old nanny would tell him off for some misdemeanor, or his mother would chase after him lovingly, or his father would tell him what a disappointment he was.

But the only ghosts were in his mind, and he tried to shut

them out as he was shown to the master bedroom—the bedroom that, in his mind, would always be his father's. The furniture was dark, the curtains heavy, and the whole room gave off a rather depressing air. If he did stay here, perhaps he would redecorate...not that he knew much about how to best decorate a home.

Or instead, he thought, he might get things in order here and then tour the properties that belonged to him around the country. It wasn't quite the same as traveling the continents, but it was better than staying in one place.

He sat down to luncheon an hour after he had arrived, and the paneled dining room felt surprisingly lonely. He hadn't realized just how used to company he had become, but then he shouldn't have been surprised. It wasn't just his time with the Lyttletons; even when he had been abroad, he had very rarely dined alone.

The soup was delicious, but the silence was stifling. As soon as he had finished, he rang the bell and asked the footman to ensure that the new man of business came to speak with him as soon as it was convenient.

The library had always been his father's domain, and even now, Colin felt a little apprehensive as he pushed open the door. This place did not seem to hold the same charm as the Lyttletons' library, but a voice at the back of his head told him that that had more to do with one regular guest of the Lyttletons' library than with the room itself.

"This house is lacking warmth," he complained to himself before calling for a fire to be built. But even once that was roaring in the grate, the room still felt cold and empty.

It did not seem to be the sort of cold that could be fixed by simply adding some heat. It needed warmth; it needed a woman's touch; it needed some life breathed into it.

Unbidden, his thoughts were filled with Susannah.

He had offended her most gravely, and he was embarrassed to even think of that night. Embarrassed...and more than a little aroused, which embarrassed him even further. She was a proper young lady, and he had no business giving in to his basest desires without first offering her marriage.

And he could not offer her marriage, no matter how often she filled his thoughts, no matter how attractive he found her, no matter how clever and intelligent and sunny she was...he could not think of her in any way but as a friend. If even that.

It was as he ate supper alone that evening that he pondered the question again: Why could he not? What was actually stopping him from asking Susannah Lyttleton to marry him and having everything he wanted?

CHAPTER TWENTY-SEVEN

COLIN LEFT THOUGHTS of marriage—and Miss Susannah Lyttleton—to marinate in his mind while he tried to focus on the issues surrounding the estate that needed to be sorted. First was a meeting with the new, younger estate manager. The man arrived early, only a day after Colin had requested the meeting, and he was polite and keen, even if he seemed extremely young.

"How has the estate been?" Colin asked once they had exchanged introductions and sat down in the study, a fresh pot of tea brought in for them.

"The estate has been well-managed in your absence, my lord. Mr. Wicks knew everyone and everything, and we were all very sad to have lost him."

Colin nodded somberly. "It is indeed a great loss," he said, reaching for his cup of tea. "It was a great comfort to know that the estate was in such good hands, even with me so far away."

"Indeed, my lord."

"But now that I am home, I need to remedy a few things. I know you have not been in the position very long, but I should like for you to tell me everything you can about the estate: what is working well, what isn't, what is profitable, and what could be improved."

They spent the next two hours poring over the accounts, with Mr. Steadman explaining the crops that would soon be harvested and what they planned to plant the following year. By the end of the meeting, Colin was pleased to have a far better understanding of how things were run and where they might increase yields or improve the conditions of the workers to make the estate more successful.

"I do not currently plan to stay here long-term," he said to Mr. Steadman. It was the first time he had said it out loud, though he had been thinking it since before he'd returned to England. He understood that he needed to act as the earl and oversee everything done in his name—but there was no reason he needed to do so from this house. He could find somewhere that would make him happier, where he could start his life in England without the ghosts of the past.

And perhaps with a wife…perhaps with Susannah.

Knowing he could not focus on work while thinking of her, he pushed her to the back of his mind and continued addressing Mr. Steadman. "Are you happy in the position? Do you think you could keep things running smoothly if I were not present?"

The young man nodded eagerly. "Oh yes, my lord. I love this job, and I'm confident I can keep everything running just the way you would like."

Colin smiled. "Excellent. Well, I think that's all for now. I have some ideas for changes I'd like to make, and I'm waiting on a letter from my lawyer about some other assets that may need my attention."

When Mr. Steadman had left, Colin looked back through the accounts one more time to ensure he truly had a handle on them. He was pleased to see that the estate was still profitable, though there were certainly areas for improvement. Funding his father's many mistresses had not bankrupted the Bourne estates, and Colin was taking steps to ensure that the estate would continue to support future earls, their families, and all the tenants who relied on it for work and a home.

Things with the estate were certainly not as problematic as his aunt had led him to believe. Yes, the complicated housing arrangements his father had left unresolved needed sorting, and Colin was the only one with the authority to do so. But other than that, things seemed to be running fairly smoothly. There was no immediate danger to the finances. And although the estate manager was young, he was clearly very enthusiastic and capable. Colin had respected old Mr. Wicks, but the man had certainly been his father's employee, not his. They had communicated occasionally through letters, and while Mr. Wicks had always done as he was bid, Colin had the sense he did not do so with the same confidence he had when it was Colin's father giving the orders.

So perhaps a new, young face was the right choice for a man Colin would likely be working with for a long time to come.

The sun was shining, though the air was chilly, so Colin decided to get out of the old house for a walk after such a busy morning of staring at figures. He strolled gently, with no destination in mind, and ended up by the fountain in the far east corner of the garden.

He smiled to himself. He remembered when his mother had commissioned the fountain and her joy at the water bubbling out of the fish's mouth in the center. She had taken such joy in little things that it was all the more terribly sad she had found so little happiness in her marriage, in her daily life.

Could he make Susannah happy? The question filled his mind. He was attracted to her, and he missed her, and he thought she would make him happy. But was he the right man for her?

He pondered this as he took supper alone, and as he lay in bed, staring up into the darkness, unable to sleep.

She loved to read, and he was content for her to spend her days lost in a book. She did not particularly enjoy society, but he was quite happy to spend their time traveling, or somewhere in the countryside. Would she enjoy travel? He knew she didn't enjoy society events and he himself only attended society functions because it was expected of him, not because he had some great love for them.

She responded passionately when she kissed him, and he was confident they would be compatible in the bedchamber. In fact, he found himself imaging her naked in his bed, her shiny brown hair loose and streaming across the pillows, her cheeks—and perhaps the rest of her, too—flushing red as he showed her the pleasures they could share.

Yes, he thought he could make her happy—and he grew more and more confident with every passing minute that she was the right women to be his countess.

Who cared if she was shy, or if she wasn't the traditional choice? And who cared if his aunt didn't find her beautiful, or even a good choice for a countess—in her estimation. He was the one who would be marrying, and as far as he was concerned, Susannah was the best choice, for him. After all, he had no wish to be a traditional earl.

And he had no wish to continue without her by his side.

CHAPTER TWENTY-EIGHT

"THAT'S IT, STAND up straight, like you're proud to be here. There's no need to hide away in the corner—you won't find a husband there."

Susannah tried to follow her mother's instructions, but all she wanted to do was disappear into the background. The knowledge that Lord Bourne had found her so unattractive only lowered her already fragile self-esteem, and she could hardly believe that any man in the room tonight would be interested enough to ask her to dance, let alone want anything more.

But her mother was insistent: *this* was the Season in which she was going to find a husband, and nothing Susannah did would deter her from her mission.

"There's definitely more interest in you tonight, with Lord Bourne gone, and your name mentioned in the society papers."

Susannah cringed at the thought. She did not like being the subject of gossip, but she supposed her mother was right; there did seem to be more gentlemen looking in her direction than usual.

She just wished she could muster some enthusiasm for them. Perhaps her life would be better once she was married. Maybe she wouldn't feel the same rush of need she had felt with Colin, but then, maybe she would. She was hardly an expert in matters of the heart. Perhaps whatever she and Colin had shared—or almost shared—was more commonplace than she'd thought. If she just found an appropriate man, maybe she could forget all the pain in her heart.

She forced herself to smile, and not long after, a middle-aged gentleman approached and made an enthusiastic bow. He had a fiercely round belly and in his waistcoat of bright red velvet, he rather reminded Susannah of an apple with a head instead of a stem, and sticks beneath for legs.

"Mr. and Mrs. Lyttleton," he said with a cloying smile. "How delightful to see you again."

"And you, Mr. Smith," they responded with almost-relieved expressions.

He turned his attention to Susannah. She did not like his leering smile or the way his eyes darted to the low neckline of her dress. It made her want to cover up, but there was no way to do so without being obviously rude. She considered whipping out her fan, but she knew her mother would have something to say about that.

"And this must be your charming daughter," Mr. Smith said.

"Please, allow me to present Miss Susannah Lyttleton," her mother said, giving her a gentle push so that she stepped forward, directly beneath Mr. Smith's gaze. His hair was not quite red but not quite blond, and in the warm room, his rounded cheeks were rather ruddy.

"A pleasure to make your acquaintance, Miss Lyttleton," Mr. Smith said with another bow, more of a bend of his spindly legs as he couldn't exactly bend his plump torso.

Still, she needed to be polite. Susannah curtsied, thanked him, and hoped she wasn't expected to engage him in further conversation.

"Like me, Mr. Smith has built his fortune in trade. He's a very successful man," her father said.

Susannah nodded and opened her mouth to extend some pleasantry, but apparently Mr. Smith wasn't interested in anything she had to say. Instead, he turned back to her father.

"Well, I'm pleased to share some business contacts with you,

Mr. Lyttleton. It is good to find someone in society who understands how money is made and isn't snobbish about whether wealth is inherited or earned. It's all the same at the end of the day, eh?"

Her father smiled and heartily agreed. But it was too soon for Susannah to feel relaxed; the man turned back to her. "Miss Lyttleton, may I have the pleasure of the next dance?" Mr. Smith asked.

Susannah did not find the man appealing in the slightest. If she was going to try to find a husband, she knew she could not be too picky—but this man was entirely wrong for her, she was sure.

Still, she could not refuse such a request, especially with her parents standing right there. They seemed rather keen for her to dance with him, which did not surprise her. He was at least ten years her senior, but what did that matter? He was clearly a good business contact and a man who would not balk at the fact that the Lyttletons did not have inherited wealth.

If only those things made Susannah happy, too.

"Of course she would," her mother said before Susannah could respond.

"Yes, thank you, Mr. Smith," Susannah agreed, dreading the prospect but knowing she would have to dance with many men to find one who could possibly be suitable.

Finding a man who not only wanted to wed her, but also inspired some desire in her seemed like a rather impossible task.

CHAPTER TWENTY-NINE

COLIN SAT DOWN at his desk and pulled out several sheets of parchment. He was not one for writing lengthy letters, even though one might think that with all his time spent abroad, he would have gotten into the habit.

He only wrote when it was necessary: figures in ledgers, brief notes to explain where he was headed. But now he felt the need to apologize, to explain. Because, try as he might, he could not get Miss Susannah Lyttleton out of his mind. And he wasn't sure he ever would.

He didn't know when it had changed from being an interest in her to being something that consumed him. Looking back on his actions, he felt terrible. His behavior had been appalling, and he could not blame her for not wanting to listen to his apology. But he needed to tell her. He needed to know if there was any way she could forgive him...and perhaps whether she felt anything real for him after weeks of pretending they were enamored with one another.

He pulled out his quill and dipped it in ink, hoping the words would come to him.

Dear Miss Lyttleton, he wrote, then struck a line through it. *Dear Susannah...* That sounded better, but perhaps it was too informal for the brief relationship they had shared, especially since he was hoping to earn her forgiveness.

He crumpled the parchment and threw it in the direction of

the fireplace, missing his target by several inches.

The fresh sheet of paper before him seemed to taunt him. What did he want to say?

I'm sorry. That was the main thing. I've been a fool… and I think I might be in love with you.

His heart began to pound erratically in his chest. He had not considered that before. That this feeling, this longing for her— could it be love?

But what else could it be?

When he rested his quill upon the parchment again, words began to flow. But they were not the ones in his mind; instead, they were those of a story. A story in which a foolish man does not realize what he has until it is too late. A story in which the perfect woman is right in front of him, and yet somehow he and all of society miss it.

He had never written a story in his life, and he had not intended to start now. But the words poured from his quill, and the more he wrote, the more it seemed like the perfect way to express what he was feeling to Miss Lyttleton. After all, she loved to read and write. Surely, it was the medium she would understand the most.

He did not realize how long he had been at his desk until there was a knock on the door, and the footman politely informed him that supper was ready.

He stretched out his hand, which felt rather cramped after gripping the quill for so long, and wrote the final line of his story, a line of dialog he hoped he would be brave enough to repeat in person when he saw Susannah again:

"Will you marry me?"

It was the only way he could see his life going now. He didn't want to be without her, and he realized that he didn't care where they settled—as long as they were together.

He didn't want to stay locally forever. The grand dining room, which was far too big for him alone, only reminded him of that. He had no wish to stay in this house, but if she wanted to, he would. He had no desire to live in London, but if she wanted to, he would.

Everything had changed so drastically since he had come to London, since he had returned to England. On the boat, he had not even been able to imagine wanting a wife, let alone feeling like he could not live without one. He had thought that someday it would just become the next task on his list. Someday in the future, when everything was in order, when he had laid the ghosts of his father's past to rest, and he had found a woman suited in every way to being a countess.

He smiled to himself as he ate the pie that Cook had prepared. Susannah was not perfectly suited to being a countess. She didn't care for society, she didn't enjoy shopping for fine clothes or gossiping with other women. She liked to hide away from the world, instead of being the focus of attention.

And yet, for him...she was the perfect countess. The only choice.

He just hoped he could persuade her of that.

WITH A SATISFIED flourish, Susannah reached the end of her story. It was only short—nothing like the length of the novels she devoured—but it was the first piece she had ever completed from start to finish.

It had not erased the terrible sadness she felt at Colin's leaving, at him finding her so woefully unattractive.

But it had at least taken her mind off it. She had snatched every moment she could in the week since he had left, scribbling away and breaking more quills than she could count. Her mother had commented on the ink stains covering her fingers and the amount of time she was spending writing rather than reading. But as long as Susannah attended every function requested of her— having scrubbed the ink thoroughly from her fingers—her mother seemed to accept that whatever she was doing was not a problem.

With a sigh, Susannah slid the sheaf of parchment into the drawer of her bureau and locked it. She had no plans to show it to anyone. Her parents would surely think it ridiculous. And she was not brave enough to submit it to a magazine.

She thought she might have shown Colin, for he had seemed so interested in her…but he had probably just been feigning that as well. Besides, she would hate to be laughed at—and he would surely think it ridiculous that she thought her words might be important. That she hoped they might give someone else the same sort of escape the words of Miss Austen or others gave to her.

For now, the words would remain hidden in a drawer, known only to her.

CHAPTER THIRTY

S HE WAS READING in the parlor when her mother came in with a determined look on her face.

"Susannah, please put the book down. I wish to speak with you."

Susannah placed the silk ribbon she always used as a bookmark in the novel, and closed it carefully.

"Yes, Mama?"

"We have three events left this Season. You have been more successful than in previous Seasons, but you still have no offers of marriage."

"I am sorry, Mama." Susannah looked down at the floor. She didn't need her failings drawn to her attention; she was well aware of them.

"Do you wish to get married?" her mother asked.

Susannah paused before answering. Before this Season, her honest answer would probably have been no. She hadn't had any wish to move, to have to conform to someone else's expectations of how she ought to behave. But now, since Colin… Something had awoken in her that she hadn't known existed. Something sinful—but something she wanted to feel again, some day. And as it obviously was not going to be with Colin, she needed to find another man who could inspire similar feelings.

If she wanted to live her life as she wished, she needed a husband—one who wouldn't try to change the person she was.

But she thought that he would probably be quite difficult to find.

"Yes," she said quietly.

"Well, that's something," Mama said. "Papa has arranged for some gentlemen to come to dinner on Friday. I need you to be at your very best—for any one of them would make a fine husband. I do not want you to regret not making an effort and ending up as a spinster, Susannah."

She reached out and patted Susannah's hand, and Susannah knew she was trying to be kind, even though it was painful to know that these prospective men surely knew why they were being invited to dinner, and quite probably had only been persuaded to attend by her dowry.

She couldn't do anything about their motivation, but she could change her own attitude, she told herself once her mother had gone. They might be interested in her dowry initially, but she could surely win them over.

She just needed to see which of the gentlemen attending seemed the most likely to let her spend her days as she pleased, and then ensure he asked her to marry him.

It couldn't be so difficult…could it?

COLIN'S HEART WAS lighter on the journey back to London than it had been leaving it. He had thought that leaving felt wrong because he had no wish to return to his childhood home, and while there was some truth in that, he now realized it hadn't been the main reason for his despair.

It had felt wrong to leave Susannah—and now that he was returning, everything seemed better.

He had decided to take a horse, rather than slowing the journey down with a carriage. He was quite happy to spend two days in the saddle, and he didn't need to bring much with him. He would have to stop at an inn for night, to allow his horse to rest, although he doubted he would manage to sleep himself. He even told his valet to stay behind. This was a journey he wanted to make quickly, and alone.

If all went well, his life would have an entirely different course by the time he was ready to leave.

And if it did not…well, he would return to Kent and deal with his emotions there.

The story he had written was tucked carefully in his saddle-bag, and he hoped it would help him explain how he felt when he actually came face to face with her. He did not think these words should be delivered by a messenger—and he didn't think he'd have the patience to wait for her response, anyway. It needed to be in person, and it needed to be as soon as possible.

He rode hard and fast, the wind rushing through his hair, probably tangling his accursed curls, and tried to ignore the nerves churning in his stomach. She had been the one to tell him to go…what if she did not wish to see him?

But, he reasoned with himself, he had not told her then how he felt. That he wanted to marry her. That he had lost his head, and his heart, to her, and he could not think of anyone else.

Surely that had to make a difference?

"LORD PENDLETON, A pleasure to see you again," Susannah's father said, as the third and final gentleman of the evening arrived. Mr. Gregor had been first, a full fifteen minutes early, followed by Mr. Jefferson, and now the most distinguished guest—Baron Pendleton—was nearly twenty minutes late.

"Thank you for the invitation," Susannah heard Lord Pend-leton say, as her father showed him into the dining room. It was a rather awkwardly numbered table, with so many gentlemen, but her mother had made it clear that she didn't want there to be any other female vying with Susannah for the men's attention.

"May I introduce my wife and my daughter, Miss Susannah Lyttleton," Papa said, and Lord Pendleton gave a stiff bow. He was definitely older than Susannah, with thinning gray hair and a bushy mustache. The seat beside Susannah had been especially saved for him, with the other two gentlemen sitting opposite, and as he sat, Susannah reminded herself that she needed to choose one of these men and look for the positives. She'd start with Lord Pendleton's kind eyes.

She wasn't going to go into the next Season still searching for a husband.

"Have you enjoyed the Season, Miss Lyttleton?" Mr. Jefferson asked. He was probably the youngest of the three, although still several years older than Susannah, she was fairly sure. He had reddish hair and a habit of clearing his throat regularly.

"Yes, thank you," Susannah said, because it seemed like the right answer, even if it wasn't wholly true. There had certainly been parts of the Season she had enjoyed...and parts she had hated.

"Have you found it pleasant?" she asked, trying to keep the conversation flowing. She saw her mother smile out of the corner of her eye and was pleased that she seemed to be doing the right thing, for once.

"I must admit, I prefer the countryside. I like to hunt and fish—and I miss both while in the city."

"But London has so much to offer!" Mr. Gregor said. He had sandy hair tied back in a queue, and the buttons of his waistcoat were straining slightly. "There is so much society has to offer. It is London I miss when everyone returns to the countryside."

"And do you enjoy the countryside or the city better, Lord Pendleton?" Susannah asked. She wished she found making conversation easier with these men, but she could not think of anything else to say. It felt like such an effort, and she only hoped it would get easier with time. So far, she was not sure which of the gentlemen seemed like the best candidate to pursue.

"I find the city more stimulating," Lord Pendleton said. "In fact, I may remain in the city once the Season has ended."

Her father took over the topic of the conversation, and Susannah took the opportunity to consider each of the men. She wondered why Lord Pendleton planned to remain in the city, for it was not the normal course of events. She wondered if his country home was not in a good state—although, of course, he wouldn't mention that. She did not like knowing that these gentlemen were quite probably only here because of the size of her dowry. They were probably in desperate need of funds—and so her only appeal was the money attached to her.

They knew so much more about her than she was likely to be able to find out about them, and it seemed rather unfair that she needed to choose a husband with so little information.

The footman entered with the next course, followed by the butler, who went straight to Papa and indicated that he needed to speak with him. Susannah saw her father frown at whatever this new information was, and then he stood.

"Please excuse me a moment," he said, following the butler from the room.

Susannah tried to catch her mother's eye to see if she knew what was happening, but her mother smoothly carried on the conversation.

"We have fantastic grounds for hunting," Mama said. "Perhaps you can join us sometime, Mr. Jefferson. And Lord Pendleton and Mr. Gregor, too, if you are also interested in the hunt."

"That sounds delightful," Mr. Gregor said with a grin. "Do you like to ride, Miss Lyttleton?"

Susannah struggled with whether to be honest or not. On one hand, she was supposed to be making a good impression. But on the other, it did not seem like a particularly early auspicious way to start a potential courtship if she was completely lying about who she was and what she enjoyed.

"It is not my favorite pastime," she admitted and noticed her mother frowning.

"But you are a very accomplished rider, dear," her mother said, her tone a little forced.

"And what is it you enjoy doing?" Mr. Jefferson asked.

She felt she had to be honest and so replied, "I really enjoy reading."

"How charming," Mr. Gregor said. "Although I must say, reading has never greatly appealed to me. There are so many other things to spend one's time on, don't you agree?"

"Indeed," Susannah said, although she clearly did not agree. Why would she have said she loved to read if she thought there were so many better options available? The man seemed a fool.

The door to the dining room reopened, and her father came back in. "Apologies for disturbing the meal, but Susannah, I must speak with you for a moment, please."

Susannah put down her knife and fork, wondering what she had done wrong. She could not imagine a reason her father would call her out of a meal with such important guests—especially when the point of the meal was to find her a husband.

The gentlemen around the table rose as she did, and she hurried to follow her father, her mind racing.

"Is aught amiss, Papa?" she asked once the heavy dining room door had closed behind them.

Her father shook his head.

"Not exactly amiss. But there is someone here to see you, and I think it only right that you see him immediately."

Now she was even more confused. Unless the king had awoken from his madness and decided to pay a call upon her, she could not imagine whom her father would deem important enough to interrupt dinner.

But her father was simply hurrying ahead, and so she followed, keen to find out who this mystery man was and what made him so important.

CHAPTER THIRTY-ONE

COLIN KNEW IT was not a polite hour of the day to be paying social calls, but he could not wait. He had ridden here in such haste, and there was no way he could wait until an acceptable hour for calling the following morning to see her—to tell her what was in his heart.

Mr. Lyttleton had been surprised to see him, that much had been clear from his expression. When he had asked to see Susannah, her father had said she was entertaining guests for dinner. Colin had strained to hear the voices in the dining room, and when he had heard at least two different male voices, jealousy filled his chest.

"I need to see her," he'd said to Mr. Lyttleton. "Please, it will not take long."

And thankfully Mr. Lyttleton had not argued any further, and had gone to fetch her—leaving Colin in the library, of all places, pacing, his body full of nervous energy, the story he had written in his pocket.

It felt stupid now. He was a grown man, an earl; why had he written some silly story to tell her how he felt? He should just tell her he hadn't been able to stop thinking about her since he had left London…

He only hoped Mr. Lyttleton trusted his integrity enough—however misplaced that trust might be—to leave them alone for a few moments. He could not tell her this in front of her father, or her mother. Perhaps he might manage in front of her maid, if that was the only choice.

If she said yes, then he wouldn't have to worry about being chaperoned with her again. They could be together, just like they had been in this very library—but without having to worry about being caught.

⟫⟫⟫⟪⟪⟪

WHEN SHE RECALLED the moment in years to come, Susannah would swear that her heart had stopped when she entered the library and saw him there.

It was almost as if he were a vision she had conjured simply by thinking about him too much. And for him to be here, now, in this place where so much had happened…and when she had been trying to decide which of the men in the dining room could possibly inspire a similar feeling within her…well, it did not seem real.

And yet it was. She had thought she would never see him again, though here he was, not even a fortnight after he had left.

Her mouth went dry, her eyes met his, and she very belatedly curtsied.

"Lord Bourne," she managed to say, even though her heart was screaming, *Colin*.

"Miss Lyttleton," he said, with a bow of his head. "I apologize for interrupting your evening. I just wish to speak to you for a moment…"

He glanced at her father, and she wondered if Papa knew what this was about. Surely he was not going to leave them alone?

For Susannah knew they could not be trusted unchaperoned.

"I must not leave our guests," Papa said, his eyes darting toward the door. "But I trust you won't be long. And the footman is only on the other side of the door, understood?"

Susannah felt her cheeks flush red, but Colin merely nodded and calmly said, "Thank you, Mr. Lyttleton. I assure you this won't take long."

And then they were alone. The doors were open, and the footman was only yards away…but they were alone.

Susannah did not know what to say. She couldn't tell him that she'd missed him. And it felt rude to ask why he was there—though she was desperate to know. She had been the one who had told him to leave, and he had left without a fight. Surely he could not be here out of guilt over what had almost happened between them?

"I—" Lord Bourne began to speak, and then stopped just as suddenly, seemingly as awkward in this situation as she was. He rummaged in his pockets and pulled out a creased piece of parchment, which, on closer inspection, seemed to be multiple pieces of parchment, all filled with writing.

He handed them to her, and she could not help but notice that his hands were shaking as he did so.

"What is this?" she asked, taking it from him, more curious than she had ever been in her life.

"Please, just read it," he said, and she did not think she could deny him anything—not when he looked at her like that, his beautiful eyes wide and pleading, his usual confidence absent.

And so she began to read. It became clear fairly quickly that this was a story, but who had written it and why was not obvious. She read as quickly as she could, very aware of him watching her as she did so. Had he written this? And if so, why was he giving it to her?

She quickly became absorbed in the tale. It was a simple story of a man not realizing he loved the woman right in front of him, and it culminated in him asking her to marry him.

"Did you write this?" she asked, looking up and meeting his sparkling blue eyes.

He nodded.

"I don't…" She bit her bottom lip. She did not understand the meaning of this, of him coming all this way with a story he had written. Was it simply to make a joke of the fact that she wished to be a writer, or that she clearly had feelings with him, when he was not attracted to her?

"Are you mocking me?" she asked, holding her head as high as she could.

His eyes widened. "Never."

"You made it perfectly clear you are not attracted to me," she said, even though it physically hurt to say the words. "So I do not comprehend why you would give me this, why—"

He took a step towards her and took both her hands in his, crumpling the parchment between their fingers. "That is not true," he said in an urgent whisper. "I *am* attracted to you. I have been…for quite some time."

"But that night, in this very room, you—" She kept her voice low, for fear that the footman on the other side of the door would hear and know what they were discussing. "You said you could not…"

CHAPTER THIRTY-TWO

H E HAD NOT realized just how badly she had misinterpreted his actions. She'd thought he was not attracted to her, when that could not have been further from the truth. The hurt in her eyes made so much more sense now, and he hated himself yet again, and hated that she so easily believed that he did not want her.

He wanted her more than he had ever wanted anything in his life.

"The only reason I said that, why I stopped, was because I could not be that man. I would not be like my father, with illegitimate children and—" He cut himself off, not wanting to ruin this moment with talk of such unsavory topics.

"Susannah. I am in love with you. I do not know when precisely I fell in love, but I am here now to tell you I have been a blind fool. You are beautiful, a rare jewel, and I wrote that story to try to convey to you exactly how I feel because I was afraid I wouldn't have the right words to give you when we spoke. And I wanted to make sure to tell you..." He took a deep breath. She was looking at him like he was speaking a foreign language that she could not understand, and yet he had to finish what he was saying, had to make his feelings clear. He dropped to his knee. "To ask if you would do me the honor, the very great honor, of becoming my wife."

THERE WAS SINCERITY in his eyes, and yet Susannah could not believe what he was saying. It had to be some joke, some prank, a lie. There was no way a man like Lord Bourne could think she was attractive, could believe himself in love with her.

Things like that only happened in stories, not in real life.

"You cannot be in love with me," she said with a nervous laugh. "It just…it can't be true. Look at me, and look at you. We struggled enough to make people believe we were courting for a reason. I am plain and simple, and I know that. I realize you must have an inkling of my feelings, and that is why you are here—because you are a good man—but—"

He gripped her hands tightly. "I had no notion of your feelings until this very moment, and even now I'm not clear. You told me to leave, and if you still wish me to, I will not impose my presence upon you. But if what I have said changes anything…"

Susannah felt like her cheeks were on fire. "I am sure you are aware that I have been attracted to you since the moment I first saw you."

A smile spread across his handsome face. "I did not know that," he said, still holding her hands tightly, still so close. "And could I dare hope that these feelings might extend beyond simple attraction?"

Susannah bit her bottom lip and tried to make sense of everything that was happening. She knew, better than she knew anything else in her life, that she felt far more for him than mere attraction. What she was feeling might well be love…but if she declared it, and this was all some elaborate prank—or even if it was just Colin trying to be kind, without realizing how much it would hurt to have such hope pulled away—then she would rather keep her feelings to herself.

"You cannot be in love with me," she repeated, struggling to maintain eye contact with him and yet unable to tear her gaze away.

Her parents would surely be wondering where she was. Perhaps they would come looking for her. And there were three gentlemen in the dining room they were expecting her to converse with and entertain and quite possibly choose from to marry.

But Colin was here, in the library, telling her words she could not believe but had longed to hear.

"I can, and I am, Susannah. You think yourself so plain and ordinary because that is what you have been told all your life. But I see the real you, and I love you. I love *you*—not some version of you that you are trying to display to the world, not your dowry, or your father's connections. I love you—and if you think there's any chance you could love me back, I am begging you to marry me."

And with such a heartfelt declaration, what could she do but agree?

"If you are sure...if this is real...then yes, I will marry you, Colin."

HE HAD THOUGHT she hated him for that night in the library, when he had taken things too far, when he had almost ruined her. He had thought that was the reason she had sent him away.

But instead, it seemed she simply believed him indifferent to her. He had not expected to have to persuade her that what was between them was real, but when she finally accepted it, it was all the sweeter.

When she agreed to become his wife, he pulled her to him, not caring that they were in the parlor and that anyone could walk in, or that the footman was just outside the door, and pressed his lips to hers. She melted beneath his touch, and once again the thought came to him of what she would be like when he could really show her what pleasure love had to offer.

It was a night he could not wait for—their wedding night. And he was certainly going to make sure it took place as soon as possible.

He lost himself in the kiss, her lean frame pressed against his body, her arms around his neck, pulling him closer, as their tongues danced and desire filled his body.

As always seemed to be the case with Susannah, and in this room, he was losing control, losing his sense of propriety. Had a voice not interrupted them, he could not have said what would have happened next.

He rather thought that he might have anticipated their wedding vows earlier than expected.

"Susannah, you really must—" Mr. Lyttleton's voice cut off abruptly as he entered the room and encountered the scene before him. Colin and Susannah pulled apart hastily, and Colin was sure his face was as flushed as hers, his lips swollen, his eyes full of desire.

"Now, look here," Mr. Lyttleton began, clearly thinking that he did not care whether Colin was a lord or not—this pushed his hospitality to the limit.

"I apologize profusely for disturbing your dinner party," Colin said swiftly, before Mr. Lyttleton could say something he might regret, or even throw him out. "I have just asked Miss Lyttleton for her hand in marriage, and I am delighted to say she has accepted. I hope we have your blessing. I can only apologize for not asking you first."

Mr. Lyttleton's mouth opened and closed several times without any sound coming out, as if all words had been lost to him.

Colin reached out and took Susannah's hands. "I do not wish to spoil your evening, but perhaps we might tell Mrs. Lyttleton the good news before I depart."

"Of—of course, Lord Bourne," Mr. Lyttleton said, hurrying from the room.

Colin turned back to Susannah, whose eyes were full of joy,

and beamed.

"You're sure?" she asked, and he hated how little confidence she had in herself, in his love.

He would spend the rest of his life proving to her how much she meant to him.

"More sure than I have ever been about anything in my life."

When Susannah's parents reentered the library, it was clear by the look on Mrs. Lyttleton's face that she had been told something of the reason for her summons. Her eyes darted between Colin and Susannah, and when Susannah did not seem able to say anything, Colin took the lead.

"I am very pleased to inform you that Susannah has agreed to become my wife."

Mrs. Lyttleton clapped her hands together in glee, and a smile spread across her face. "Lord Bourne, what wonderful news. And Susannah! You shall be a countess!"

CHAPTER THIRTY-THREE

IT WAS ON a sunny Wednesday, only a week after Lord Bourne's arrival, that Susannah and Colin were wed. He had insisted on procuring a special license, and Susannah had no reason to argue.

She didn't think she would believe it was all real until they exchanged vows, and she was officially his wife.

Wife. Countess. It was hard to imagine herself when she thought of those labels. For her entire life she had been Miss Susannah Lyttleton, the plain, bookish daughter of a merchant.

And now she was to become Lady Bourne.

If she'd read it in a novel, she would have laughed it off as unbelievable. And yet here she was, on the day of her wedding, the rest of her life before her.

"Thank you, Louise," Susannah said, as her maid finished pinning her mousy brown hair into a chignon, leaving a few loose curls to frame her face.

"It's time to put your dress on, Miss Lyttleton," her maid said. "There's not long before we need to leave."

Susannah nodded. She had been waiting until the last possible moment to put on her dress, because she was so worried about ruining it. She would have been happy to wear her Sunday best, but Colin had insisted that she have a new gown, and that it be white, since Princess Charlotte's wedding dress had been.

Susannah did not think she ought to be even suggesting a

comparison between herself and the princess, but Colin had ordered the dress and paid for it, and she had to admit it was a thing of beauty. Far too beautiful for her to wear, which was why she had waited to put it on until she could wait no longer.

It was trimmed with lace, and when she slipped it on, she felt like she was someone else. Like… a princess. Louise held out the white gloves for her to slip on, and then she turned and looked at herself in the mirror.

Her eyes were bright, her cheeks rosy, and a smile played upon her lips.

This was her wedding day.

It was a day she had thought might never come, and yet here it was. And the man who would be waiting at the church for her was Colin, an earl, and a man she had lost her heart to.

She did not think it was possible to be happier than she was in that moment.

"You look beautiful, Miss Lyttleton," Louise said, and for once, Susannah felt it. Oh, she knew her features were not perfectly symmetrical, and her brown hair and brown eyes would always be rather ordinary. But for a brief moment she saw what Colin said he saw, and it filled her with joy.

There was a knock on the door and, without waiting for a response, her mother entered the room. In the mirror, Susannah saw her stop at the sight of her daughter. She turned to face her, feeling rather self-conscious.

"Is it time to go?" she asked.

Her mother nodded. "Yes. The carriage is waiting outside. You look… Goodness, Susannah. I have never seen you looking quite so radiant."

"Thank you, Mama."

"This is an excellent match, of course—but I think it is a love match, too."

Susannah had not yet told Colin she loved him. She knew in her heart it was true, but she had not been alone with him since that evening in the library, when he had declared himself. And it hadn't been something she was comfortable saying when her mother or her maid was chaperoning.

She would tell him that evening, she had decided. On their wedding night...a night which filled her with anticipation and nerves.

"It is, Mama," she said softly. "And I couldn't be happier."

"Well, your father and I are thrilled for you both, my dear," she said, reaching out to squeeze Susannah's gloved hand. "And now we must leave, before your groom thinks you have changed your mind!"

Susannah was more concerned that he might change his mind. He had declared his love for her in the strongest terms, and yet she still could not quite believe it to be true. She kept waiting for the catch, and yet here they were, on their wedding day, without any sign of the other shoe dropping.

As she walked down the staircase, she remembered seeing Colin waiting there, the first time they had attended a ball together. She wished he was there now, for his presence often settled her nerves, just as much as it riled her emotions.

In a few short hours, she would be his wife, and they would leave this house together. She did not know where they were to go, but he'd said he had a plan, and she found she trusted him implicitly.

And tonight...tonight she would discover what could have happened in the library, if he had not been worried about becoming a man like his father.

She knew it was probably sinful, but she could not wait to feel his hands on her body once more, to chase that fiery pleasure and find out where it led.

"You look very flushed, Susannah," her mother said as they stepped into the carriage. "Do you feel well?"

"Yes, Mama," Susannah said, feeling her cheeks redden even further. If she was to make it through the wedding ceremony and breakfast without looking like a fool, she needed to control her thoughts a little better.

But it was so difficult, when she had thought of him for months, and believed that her dreams could never become a reality…

THE ONLY GUEST Colin had invited was his aunt, who had opposed the match, but did not seem inclined to make a fuss. When he had announced the betrothal, she had reiterated that Susannah was a nice young lady—but that she had her concerns about her ability to be a countess.

And Colin had told her that he was in love with Miss Susannah Lyttleton, and that he did not care whether or not she was born to be a countess. She was the woman he wanted as his wife, and therefore she would be the next Lady Bourne.

He stood at the front of the small church and waited for his bride and her parents to arrive. He was slightly worried that she wouldn't show up. He was fairly confident that she *wanted* to marry him. But he still wasn't sure that she believed he loved her.

He would have wed her sooner, but he had wanted her to have something special to be married in, and a week was the quickest the modiste could have it ready. Thankfully, her parents had not argued when he had said he wished to procure a special license, rather than waiting for the banns to be read.

Considering the kiss Mr. Lyttleton had walked in on, he wondered if they realized that it was prudent for the two to be wed sooner rather than later. Colin was resolute in not lying with Susannah until they were wed, but he did not feel the need to put temptation in his way by making them wait a month or more to marry.

It had seemed silly to open up his London house for a week, so instead he had stayed with his aunt on the outskirts of London, in order to avoid any late night library moments with Susannah.

But tonight…tonight everything would change.

And he wasn't apprehensive at all. He worried that she might not turn up, but he was not worried about their marriage. He was confident he would remain faithful to her until his dying day, and that she would be the woman to fill his heart and his home with happiness.

When the church doors opened, Colin had almost persuaded himself that she wasn't going to come. His mouth was dry and his pulse racing, and when he set eyes on her, his heart felt like it might burst.

She was beautiful. Resplendent in white lace, the sun behind her made her look like some kind of angel. The joy in her face could not be denied, and as she walked towards him, she seemed to walk taller and straighter, as though she was just as sure about this as he was.

CHAPTER THIRTY-FOUR

SUSANNAH REPEATED THE words as she was instructed, but she could not focus on them for long enough to remember them. This handsome earl was to be her husband, and her thoughts were as jumbled by the sight of him as they had been on the first day she had met him.

When he placed the wedding band on her finger, and she knew she truly belonged to him, she almost wept with joy.

"HOW DO YOU feel, Lady Bourne?" Colin asked, and Susannah giggled. She could not believe that title could possibly belong to her. They sat beside each other in the coach, close but not touching, and although Susannah rather wished to reach out to him for reassurance, she didn't yet feel able.

Thankfully, he did. He took her hand and held it within his as the carriage rattled back to the Lyttletons' London home.

"I feel...elated, and excited, and nervous, and like I can't really believe any of this is happening."

He took her gloved hand and pressed it to his lips, and a shiver went through her body even though he had not made contact with her skin. It felt like a promise of so much more to come.

"I feel exactly the same. And I hope you will be pleased with the plans I have made for after the wedding breakfast."

"I do not believe I could feel anything other than joy today, Colin," Susannah said, her heart near to bursting with joy.

"I do not wish to return to my house in Kent just yet. It is not a place that holds such happy memories for me, and although I am sure we will make our own, it is not where I wish to begin our married life."

"I will happily live wherever makes you happy," she said, knowing in her heart it was true. As long as he was happy, she would be too.

"We can decide where to live permanently together. But first of all… I thought we might travel a little."

Susannah could not help but smile. "You know how I have longed to see more of the world," she said, trying not to make her excitement at the prospect too obvious, though she needed him to think carefully on it. "But I thought you needed to stay in England a while? You had returned after so long abroad because your estate needed you…"

"I fear my aunt may have exaggerated the urgency of my return. I believe she thought I was living a ruinous life, as I am afraid my father did, and she was concerned that the title and the estates might pass to some distant relation if I did not do my duty."

"So she lied to you?"

"Not so much lied," Colin began, more than willing to be generous on this happy day, "but she certainly embellished a little. And in the time I have been back in England, I have managed to iron out some of the difficulties with the estates, as well as ensure the new estate manager is competent. I do not think the properties, nor the title of Bourne, will suffer overly if I take a few months to journey around Europe with my countess."

HE COULD SEE the excitement in her eyes at the prospect, and it filled him with joy. He loved to travel, and he had always assumed that once he was wed, such activity would have to come to an end.

But it seemed likely that Susannah would enjoy accompanying him if he wished to visit the Continent, or even further afield. He would not leave the country for years, as he had done as a lad of eighteen, but he certainly did not need to feel tied to England, weighed down by the estates, which held such mixed memories for him. And if he had to endure some sea-sickness in order to show her the world…well he would do so without complaint.

Susannah beamed. "Well, in that case, I would be delighted for us to travel."

"And while we are away, I thought you might gain inspiration for a full-length novel—like the ones you enjoy so much. Perhaps even something you could attempt to get published."

"Oh, I could never—" Susannah began, but Colin put a finger to her lips. The contact between his bare skin and the delicate skin of her lips made her gasp and silenced her.

"You can do anything you want, Susannah. You are an incredible woman, and I mean to show you everything that life has to offer."

No one seemed quite accustomed to Susannah's sudden change in title and status. She was called Miss Lyttleton several times by the staff until they were corrected by her mother. And Susannah herself did not immediately respond when Colin's aunt addressed her as "Lady Bourne", and she was rather taken aback when a friend of her mother's, who had joined them for the festivities, curtsied to her.

Being a countess would certainly take some getting used to.

"I should like to propose a toast," her father said, raising his glass. "To Lord and Lady Bourne. Wishing them a life full of happiness, through every season of their lives."

Susannah met Colin's eye and smiled as glasses were raised to them. She could not imagine *not* being happy with Colin. She loved him, and he loved her. It was a far better start to marriage than she could have possibly dreamed of. And he wanted to take her traveling...to broaden her horizons and allow her to see something of the world.

He even believed she could write a novel. Something people would want to read.

She wasn't sure she could ever believe in herself the way he seemed to, but she wanted to try.

CHAPTER THIRTY-FIVE

SUSANNAH SAT BEFORE the looking glass in the room they had taken at an inn on the outskirts of London, and took a deep, calming breath.

She was married. She was Lady Bourne—and her husband would soon be joining her in this bedchamber.

Every inch of her being thrummed with anticipation for the moment he would walk in the door. She knew a little of what to expect, from her reading, from a flustered conversation with her mother, and from that night in the library where things had progressed further than she had imagined…

Excitement overcame her nerves, and when he knocked gently on the door, she rushed to it and pulled it open.

He had two glasses of port, and he handed her one with a smile. "You look beautiful in that dress."

"I don't think I'll ever look *beautiful*," she said, taking the glass and sipping the ruby liquid. "But thank you."

He closed the door behind him and took a step closer, so she could almost feel the heat from his body, even through their clothing.

"You *are* beautiful," he said, his eyes darkening, and desire pooled in her belly. "And I will show you just how beautiful, every night for the rest of her lives."

Susannah felt the blood rush to her cheeks, and she took another, much larger, sip of the port, which did not help the situation.

Her mind went blank, and she finished the port just to fill the simmering silence.

He drained his own glass, only briefly breaking eye contact, and then took both glasses and put them on the table by the door. Susannah's nerves felt like elastic being stretched until it was close to snapping. He took her hand, and her breathing became shallow.

She had not removed her gloves, and so he began to do so for her, pulling at each finger and then gently sliding the satin from her skin. She gasped as he pressed a kiss to the fluttering pulse at her wrist, before repeating the action with the other glove, another kiss, and a squeak of desire from Susannah that she could not control.

"Beautiful," he murmured, before reaching up to her carefully pinned hair and pulling each pin gently from it, dropping them onto the carpet as he did so.

She could feel the blush spreading from her cheeks down to her décolletage at his focused attention, but she stood still as he removed every last one, and then allowed him to turn her around, so that she was facing the bed.

Her body shook with anticipation, and her eyes flickered closed as he pressed his lips to her neck. His fingers began to undo the shell buttons on the back of her bodice, and the dress became looser, until he could slide the sleeves from her shoulders and leave it in a pool around her feet.

And so there she stood, in only her chemise, shivering in spite of the fire roaring in the grate on the other side of the room.

His arms encircled her waist, pulling her backwards against him, and then one hand moved to cup her breast through the thin fabric.

"Beautiful," he murmured against the delicate skin of her neck, and she was glad he had hold of her waist for she was sure her knees were about to give way. The desire which raged within her felt as though it would burn her up at any moment, and when he turned her to kiss her, she wrapped her arms around his neck and held on for dear life.

JJUST AS HE had anticipated, she was deliciously responsive to his touch. He hated that she could not accept his compliment without disagreeing, and so he set out to show her just how beautiful he found her body.

When he kissed her, though, he lost sight of his aim to show her the beauty in every inch of her body, and instead found himself pulling at her chemise, separating their lips for a moment as he slipped it over her head, until she was naked before him, a goddess by the firelight.

"Beautiful," he said again, but it was almost like she only just realized she was bare, and suddenly felt the need to cover herself with her arms.

He reached for her hands, pulling them away gently, and placed them on his own shirt. She seemed to understand, and pulled it over his head, as he worked on divesting himself of his britches, a task which was becoming more challenging by the second.

He had wanted her for weeks, and the thought of her finally being his, of being able to sate his desire for her without feeling any guilt, was intoxicating.

Seeing nervousness in her eyes, he kissed her again, slowly, as though they had all the time in the world, as though his body wasn't a raging fire of desire. They somehow made it to the bed without tripping over their combined clothing, and his fingers trailed up from her creamy thighs, until he reached her breasts and slid a thumb over one nipple, causing her to gasp and her hips to buck beneath his.

"Colin," she groaned. "I need…"

"What, my love?"

"I need…you," she said, and no words had ever been so welcome.

"Do you believe you're beautiful?" he asked, unable to help himself.

"I—"

Still she did not seem to be able to say the words. He lowered his mouth to her other nipple and grazed it with his lips, provoking another delicious groan from her mouth, and then pulled away.

"Do you believe it?"

"I…"

He swept his fingers over one breast, across her stomach, and halted just above the curls between her thighs.

"I believe you think I'm beautiful," she said, the words forced from her lips in such a hurry that they seemed to meld together.

And he decided that would be enough, for now.

He moved his fingers lower, and her eyes pressed shut, and her breathing became heavier, as he showed her the pleasure he had wanted to show her since that night in the library.

Since before that, if he were honest.

IF IT WAS possible to die from pleasure, Susannah thought she might be about to do so. Her body needed him, and he seemed to know exactly what to do. The fire burning within her seemed to build until it was white hot, and impossible heat that she could not, did not want to, escape.

"Colin, please," she said, even though she did not know what she was begging for, but it seemed he did. As she crashed over the edge of the delicious precipice, she pressed her eyes closed and clung to him, waves of ecstasy taking over her entire body.

And then he covered his body with hers and she pulled him closer, their lips colliding as their bodies joined as one, and her heart felt like it might explode with all the emotions coursing through her body. Joy, lust, love…

CHAPTER THIRTY-SIX

S HE THOUGHT SHE had dozed for a while, although she had no way to tell. What she did know was that she was entirely naked, curled up against his solid body, a blanket pulled up to their waists.

He wore nothing either, and she blushed in that knowledge, even after all they had done.

"Colin?" she whispered, not wanting to move in case he was asleep.

"Yes, my love?" he mumbled. Those words again…words that filled her chest with warmth. Words that he seemed to truly mean.

"I love you." She said it softly at first, testing it out, then repeated it with far more conviction. "I love you." She thought she might have fallen in love with him the day he walked into the parlor and took her breath away. Love at first sight; it was not a notion she had believed in before.

But she could not deny its existence now.

"As I love you," Colin said sleepily, leaning his head down to press a kiss to her mussed hair.

Sighing with contentment, Susannah leaned her cheek against his chest and closed her eyes, and she drifted back to sleep with his heartbeat as her lullaby.

SUSANNAH HAD SEEMED surprised when Colin had expressed his wish to go to Vauxhall Gardens before they left on their travels.

"If it's something you really don't wish to do, I understand," Colin said as they lay together in the bed of the inn, the morning sunlight streaming through a gap in the curtains, their bodies sated, weary, and joyful.

"I don't mind," Susannah said, lazily drawing circles with one finger across his chest. How glorious it felt to be able to touch him like this whenever she liked. "I just suppose I wasn't expecting such an event. You never seemed to care greatly for society events, just like me."

"I do not," Colin agreed. "But I would like to do this, just once, before we leave for a while. If you'll indulge me?"

She tipped her head backward so that she could kiss his lips and then settled back against his chest. "Of course. Anything, my love."

He did not tell her the true reason he wished to attend, for he thought it might make her nervous or uncomfortable. And perhaps it was wrong of him, that he had a strong urge to return to the place where he and Susannah had made their silly vow of a fake courtship—in return for some peace and quiet, both from the ladies of the ton and from Susannah's parents.

He did not only wish to return, but to show the gossiping busybodies there what a love match really looked like.

He didn't imagine Susannah had even thought of such a thing, but he wanted to display her triumphantly as Lady Bourne, to silence those witches who had spoken of her so cruelly before they disappeared to enjoy each other without others around to complicate things.

He thought there was a good chance they would not return to England for several months. Perhaps longer; there was so much he wanted to show Susannah. And he wanted to leave England under no illusion that Susannah had been his choice.

And that he was wholly in love with her.

And, as she had revealed to him the night before, so was she.

Things really could not have ended more neatly.

EVEN THOUGH VISITING Vauxhall Gardens had been one of the society events Susannah had least detested, she still found her stomach filled with butterflies as they made their way across by boat. She didn't really understand Colin's desire to attend, but considering the happiness he had brought her, she had no intention of denying him anything he wanted.

Most of her belongings had been packed in trunks for their journey north and then across the sea—but she had managed to retrieve one of her more fashionable dresses. She did not want to let Colin down by looking like a dowdy maid.

He had made it clear to her on several occasions the previous evening that he found her beautiful, and she almost believed that he did. But that did not mean that society would see her through such rose-tinted glasses.

They had planned to travel abroad without servants and hire them when needed once they arrived, but Susannah had sent for Louise to come to the inn that evening, and the maid had happily done so to help her dress and fix her hair. She had not expected to be on display quite so soon, and the thought of what the gossips would have to say about the new Lady Bourne made her stomach churn.

As if reading her thoughts, Colin reached out and took her hand. "All will be well. We will see the Cascade, dance, watch the fireworks—and then tomorrow we shall depart and leave all of this behind us for the time being."

Susannah nodded. She did not want to confess her worries to him, for they seemed so silly. Did it matter what others thought of her when she was confident in his opinion of her? She had allowed their opinions to cloud her judgment, to make her believe that Colin had to be false, for no man—and certainly not one as handsome as him—could ever have considered her for a wife.

And yet he had. And she was Lady Bourne. So she knew the words of those vipers should not matter.

And yet she was rather afraid they would still hurt.

The gardens were buzzing with conversation and music and laughter, and Susannah held on tightly to Colin's arm as they moved through the crowds, making their way to procure refreshment.

Whenever they were noticed, Susannah was sure that whispering followed, but she tried to hold her head high and ignore it. She definitely heard the words *Miss Lyttleton*, and *plain*, and *surprising*—but she hoped Colin had not.

After a drink to fortify her nerves, Colin turned to her and asked, "Would you do me the honor of the next dance, Lady Bourne?"

She smiled in spite of herself at her new name and took his hand gladly. "You may have every dance," she said, and he led her onto the dance floor, where they certainly had the interest of the audience.

Once the music began, Susannah tried very hard to focus only on Colin, on the steps, on the fact that the last time she had danced with him here, she had thought he was a kind, handsome man whom she would never know better—and now she was his wife.

As they danced, it became easier to forget the crowd around them, and when the music ended, it felt as if they were the only two people there. Colin bowed to her, and she giggled and curtsied back, then threaded her arm through his, resting her head momentarily on his shoulder as they exited the dance floor.

It was then that she became aware once more of the eyes upon her and realized she was probably being far too familiar for a public setting. And yet Colin didn't seem to mind—in fact, as they approached the Cascade, he turned his head and pressed his lips briefly to the top of her hair and squeezed her hand.

"The Cascade is beautiful, is it not?" Susannah said with a sigh.

"It is," Colin agreed. "But not as beautiful as my wife."

CHAPTER THIRTY-SEVEN

FEELING COMFORTABLY FULL of sandwiches and ratafia, Susannah and Colin found a spot to watch the fireworks, surrounded by other members of the ton.

"Are you pleased we came tonight?" Colin asked as they waited in the dark.

"I am, actually," Susannah said with a smile. "I did not think I would be, but it has been very pleasant. And it's amazing how much more enjoyable such events are without the pressure to find a husband."

"It is certainly easier to relax without expecting some marriage-minded mama to jump out from any corner, ready to entrap me," he said with a laugh.

"Well, that was the point of our arrangement, was it not?"

To this, Colin nodded and then took her gloved hand, pressing it to his lips and lingering rather longer than was appropriate. "It was. But I must say the arrangement is remarkably better now there is no pretense. Now you are mine…in every way."

Susannah could not suppress a shiver at his words and at what he was hinting at, here in Vauxhall Gardens, surrounded by so many people.

She could feel her cheeks reddening and hoped the dark would hide them.

When she did not answer, he prompted her, "Do you not agree, my love?"

Susannah nodded and was rather pleased that the fireworks began at that moment, saving her from having to try to answer his words, which were laced with desire. She struggled to think of anything but him, even with the beautiful colors exploding across the sky above them.

⇶⇷

COLIN ENJOYED TEASING her, seeing the color rise in her cheeks, knowing he could affect her in such a way with just his words.

And yet, just because he enjoyed the reaction they provoked did not mean the words were not real.

The arrangement had been a good idea and had certainly made his Season in London more bearable. But this, now—being married to a woman he loved, who loved him too—was infinitely better.

"Who is that, with Lord Bourne?" Colin heard a female voice say behind him, and he stiffened slightly, not knowing if Susannah had heard it and hoping they were not about to spill hurtful words.

"She's rather striking, isn't she?"

Colin smiled to himself and strained his ears to hear the rest of the conversation. Beside him, Susannah did not seem to react, and he wondered if she was just too engrossed in the fireworks to pay attention to the gossips around her.

"That's his new wife," another voice said. "Did you not hear? It was quite the event—they courted, he left, and then returned, and they were married within a week."

"No, I must have missed that entirely," the first voice said, and then a rather loud firework muffled her next words.

"She was Miss Susannah Lyttleton," the other said, presumably in answer to a question.

"Goodness, that plain girl, the daughter of that merchant?"

"The very same."

Colin was about to turn around and inform the ladies that he could hear their conversation, to call them out on their rude comments, when the second said, "Well, marriage certainly seems to agree with her. She looks like a different woman."

"A love match, I heard. She certainly looks happy—although I think I'd look very happy if I had secured the hand of one of the most eligible, and the most handsome of the bachelors of the Season."

When the fireworks finished, Colin turned to see which women had been commenting on their marriage, but he could not make them out among the crowd. But it did not matter. He had wanted the ton to see that Susannah was a much-loved wife and a worthy countess—and he thought he had achieved his goal.

"Are you ready to go, my love?" he asked, offering his arm to her. "We have an early start in the morning. And I find I am rather eager to enjoy your company alone…"

He was close enough to her that he saw the blood rise in her cheeks and heard her shocked giggle—but she took his arm enthusiastically, and together they left Vauxhall Gardens, and the London Season, behind them.

SUSANNAH HAD NEVER particularly enjoyed traveling, but that was because it usually meant several days cramped in a coach with her mother and father, usually heading to London—a place where she knew she never really sparkled.

But this time was different. This time, she was alone with her husband, and they were on their way to start the first adventure of their married lives—a trip to Scotland, somewhere she had never been but always wanted to go. From there, they would sail to France and then decide where they would travel next.

The freedom to decide their future on a whim was rather heady. She had spent her entire life conforming to society's expectations, following the rules—perhaps with the exception of her mother's rule about not reading by candlelight—and knowing her days followed a predictable rhythm, dictated by the Season and the inevitable hunt for a husband.

But now that she was married, everything was different. With a husband like Colin, who wanted to see her happy and was keen to escape normal life himself, there weren't really any rules or firm plans.

"I have something for you," he said, presenting her with a parcel wrapped in tissue.

"You must stop spending money on me, Colin," Susannah said, blushing with embarrassment. He had showered her with gifts and opportunities to spend money ever since they had wed. And although she had come from a wealthy family, she had never been so spoiled.

"It is our money, and if I think it will make you happy, I will happily spend it."

"Well, I am certainly happy," Susannah said, taking the gift from him without further argument. She carefully opened the tissue and found the most beautifully bound copy of Shakespeare's *First Folio* she had ever seen.

"Colin, I do not know what to say. It is so difficult to find a copy—any copy—let alone one so exquisite as this."

"Well, it is long overdue."

Susannah frowned. "What do you mean?"

"Well, as part of our deal in Vauxhall Gardens, I promised to furnish your library with any book you desired. You have not requested one, so I used my own initiative."

"Oh, Colin," Susannah said, as tears welled up in her eyes. "You must know that you owe me nothing. That our plan in Vauxhall Gardens led us to this marriage, and for that, I could not be more content."

He smiled broadly and said, "I am glad to hear it. But I still do not like my debts to remain unpaid. And although you will not have a permanent library while we are traveling, I am sure you will acquire books...and let this be the first."

"Is there a large library at your home in Kent?" Susannah asked. They had not discussed where they would live permanently whenever they did return to England. It was another of those details that could be decided later.

"Yes. But it is not a place where I enjoy spending time. Although I am sure you could make it more enjoyable...or perhaps we will simply live elsewhere and ensure that you have the greatest library possible in our new home."

COLIN LOVED TO make Susannah smile, and he found it was surprisingly easy to do so. She was not materialistic, other than her love for books, and yet she always seemed so pleased with any trinket he bought her. He loved her, and she loved him, and that seemed to him a solid basis for a happy marriage.

One day, he was sure, they would settle in England more permanently. Perhaps once they had children—which, if their compatibility in the bedroom was anything to go by, might not be in the distant future.

He could picture himself and Susannah surrounded by a brood of children, filling a house with love, happiness, and laughter. She said she was happy, and he believed her—and he would do everything in his power to ensure she remained so until his dying day.

He had never thought that pretending to love someone could lead to the real thing, and yet here was the evidence. Of course, no one else would ever know that their courtship that Season had been false, that feelings had only become involved—well, his feelings, at least—further down the line.

And when they returned to London, he was sure gossip about the two of them would start again—about how the match had been unexpected, about how remarkable it was that Mr. Lyttleton now had a countess as a daughter.

But Colin was certain that everyone would see the love between them, for he did not think either of them could hide it— and that would surely be enough to silence their cruel tongues once and for all. It seemed to have worked in Vauxhall Gardens, after all.

And who could argue with true love, no matter where or when it struck?

EPILOGUE

"WHERE ARE WE going?" Susannah asked as their carriage continued along the road. They had been traveling for three days, and Colin had been surprisingly secretive about their intended destination.

They had seen so much of the world in the last six months—France, Spain, Italy—places Susannah had heard of but never even dreamed of seeing. Each place filled her with more inspiration, more wonder—and even getting seasick on the way home did not ruin her memories of the tour they had taken together, as the Earl and Countess of Bourne.

"You'll see," Colin said, as he had done every time she asked. Then he brought her hand to his lips and began to distract her with kisses to her wrist, to her palm, to each finger.

He was an expert at distracting her. She had been nervous about returning to England, nervous about having to face society as Lady Bourne, instead of as plain old Miss Lyttleton. Colin had told her that it did not matter what people said, that she was the countess whether they liked it or not—and that there was no one else he would have chosen but her.

But that didn't stop the butterflies from filling her stomach at the thought of entering a ballroom in London society and having everyone stare at her, everyone gossip about how surprising it had been that the Earl of Bourne had chosen such a plain miss to be his wife.

Whenever she voiced such concerns, Colin told her she was

anything but plain and proceeded to make it very clear just how attracted he was to her.

And after six months of hearing such words of endearment every single day, she tended to believe them.

But that did not stop her from being apprehensive about returning to London.

Except they did not seem to be going to London. They had landed in Plymouth, but she did not think they were on the route to the city. On the continent, he had always been excited to tell her where they were heading next, and yet this time, he was keeping it a secret. She wondered if her parents were in London or whether they were in the countryside. It felt odd, having not seen them in months, although she had exchanged regular letters with her mother. She was sure she would see them soon—and it was something she planned to discuss with Colin whenever they arrived wherever it was they were going.

COLIN STRUGGLED TO contain his excitement as the ocean came into view. He hoped this place would be everything he remembered—for there had been no chance for him to see it in person. Indeed, all the renovations and preparations had been carried out via written instructions, and so he had no idea whether things would be as he imagined.

He hoped Susannah would be pleased. There had not been a day yet, even when she had unexpectedly developed seasickness on the way home, that she had not seemed happy. She took pleasure in the small things in life, but he was still determined to make sure that their marriage was a happy one—especially for her.

He had wanted it to be a surprise. He hoped it had not been a mistake, that she would not have wanted to have input. But the memory of this place had come to him in a dream, and he had become fixated on it from that moment onward.

A trip he had taken with just his mother, to a property in Dorset. Not the finest of their homes by any means—but a place filled with light and laughter. She had taken him to the beach every day, and she had paddled in the gentle waves while he had run headlong into them, learning to swim very quickly when the first wave pulled him under.

It was a place his father had never been. A place that had never held arguments or secrets or mistresses.

And it was a place where he could easily imagine Susannah, writing happily in the library with its views of the ocean, or walking across the golden sands, perhaps with children in tow.

He would always be the Earl of Bourne, and he intended to live up to his duties—but he also craved a simpler life. One similar to the life he had lived when traveling, but with a permanent base to call his home.

And this was a place where he thought it could happen. Remote enough that they could paddle barefoot without worrying that society would be scandalized. And yet within a day's ride of London so that he could meet with his lawyer or any other businessmen whenever it was necessary.

"Is that the sea?" Susannah asked excitedly, peering out of the window of the carriage.

"It is," Colin said with a smile. "But don't worry, we are not taking another voyage on a boat. You don't need to worry about seasickness."

Susannah put a hand on her stomach. "I must say I'm rather relieved. I don't think I've quite recovered from the seasickness from that journey, even after so many days in the carriage."

"I thought we'd stay in England for the time being, if you're happy with that."

She reached out and took his hand. "I'm happy as long as I'm with you." She glanced back out of the window. "Isn't it amazing how different the color of the sea can look in different places? Here it is darker gray, perhaps a little more menacing. And yet in

Italy, it was such a vibrant blue, it almost seems like a different entity."

"You have a way of noticing things," Colin said. "I think that is what makes you such a good writer."

Susannah blushed. On the journey home, she had allowed him to read her completed novel, even though it had made her nervous to do so. She was unsurprised, though, by his compliments; she did not think he had a critical bone in his body. Well, not when it came to her, anyway—which she very much appreciated.

THE HOUSE WAS just as he remembered it—white walls and large windows, with the ocean behind it.

The coach came to a stop, and the footman opened the door, allowing Colin to climb out and then offer his hand to Susannah.

"What a beautiful place," Susannah said, keeping hold of his hand as she looked around her in awe. "Are we visiting someone?"

At this, Colin shook his head. "No. I thought, if you are happy to, we could live here…"

She turned to him, her eyes bright. "This house belongs to you?"

"To us," Colin corrected her. "I came here as a child with my mother, and I have only good memories of it. And so I thought it might be the perfect place for us to make our home—for as long as we wish to stay in one place, that is."

Susannah eagerly pulled his hand as she moved toward the doorway.

"It looks perfect, Colin. But come on, I'm desperate to see inside!"

Colin laughed at her exuberance but followed her happily, breathing in the salty air and reliving memories of his youth.

This was where he wanted to create new memories with Susannah, with his family. This was where he wanted to call home—a house full of warmth and light.

Susannah exclaimed in delight at every room they entered. When they reached the final one on the ground floor, excitement drummed through Colin's veins.

"The place has been renovated while we've been away, but I could only give instructions through letters, so I've not seen the finished outcome. But this room..." He pushed down the door handle. "This room is for you."

She stepped through the doorway and looked around in wonder. Colin couldn't help but smile. It was exactly what he had wished for.

The library had floor-to-ceiling bookshelves on every wall, most of which were filled with a carefully curated selection. There was a large fireplace for when it got cold, and a bureau in the window which overlooked the sea. A large armchair sat in the corner, and he could already picture Susannah curled up there with a book.

He wandered over to the shelf nearest him and ran his fingers across the spines.

"Oh, Colin. It's wonderful. Thank you. Thank you for...everything."

He pulled out a volume bound in green leather and turned to face her. "I have this for you, too." As he reached out to give her the book, his heart pounded in his chest.

He hoped this was not a misstep.

"You already bought me a book," Susannah said with a laugh.

"This one is special," he said, pushing the book into her hands when she didn't take it immediately.

SUSANNAH LOOKED DOWN at the green volume in her hands, and it took her a moment to realize what she was seeing. She traced over the gold letters with her finger and then looked to Colin. "This is—"

"Yours. Yes."

She looked down again at the words. *Swan Song* by Lady B.

She had never expected to see her title, her name, on the front of a book.

Just as she had never expected her name to stop being Susannah Lyttleton.

"I got this copy bound for you. For us. But I've also… I have spoken to a publisher. Anonymously, of course. And he is interested in publishing your novel—if you wish to share it with the world."

Susannah felt like she might cry. It was such a kind gesture, and it also made her feel so very nervous. She was glad that he had not sent the full manuscript off to a publisher without her knowing, for there were some tweaks she still wished to make. But to have a bound copy of it in her hands… She wondered if that might be enough to satisfy her dream. Although the thought of people across England reading her words—especially as they would not know they were her words—was rather thrilling.

"Can I…Can I think on it for a while?"

"Of course you can. I think your writing is wonderful. If you want to keep it for yourself, I would understand. And if you want to share it with the world, then I will be right behind you."

Susannah carefully placed the book down on a coffee table and then reached for her husband, pulling him into an embrace. "I don't know what I did to be so lucky to get you as a husband, but I thank God every day. But there is just one thing I must query…"

"Oh?" Colin said, raising his eyebrows. She wasn't surprised at his reaction; she had not really asked him for anything since they had wed.

"You said earlier that this was my room. But I think that is wrong."

"I had it redesigned for you, my love."

"And I love it. But I think that this library should be our room. And that we need a rug in front of the fireplace…"

Colin's eyes lit up, and he tilted her head back and pressed his lips to hers in a fiery promise of what was to come.

"I concur, Lady Bourne," he said, before sweeping her off her feet and carrying her all the way to their bedchamber upstairs.

About the Author

Daphne Quinn loves nothing more than curling up with a large cup of tea and a regency romance. She adores the drama and the dresses of the past—even though she is quite happy with all the comforts of the present! She loves living in England and visiting historic sites like the beautiful city of Bath. She shares photos of her visits—as well as upcoming releases and sales!—on her Facebook page facebook.com/authordaphnequinn.